LOVE UNDER THE OVERPASS

LOVE UNDER THE OVERPASS

Into the Refiner's Fire

M.J. ROSENKOETTER

WESTBOW® PRESS
A DIVISION OF THOMAS NELSON & ZONDERVAN

WestBow Press books may be ordered through booksellers or by contacting:

WestBow Press
A Division of Thomas Nelson & Zondervan
1663 Liberty Drive
Bloomington, IN 47403
www.westbowpress.com
1 (866) 928-1240

ISBN: 978-1-4908-2167-2 (e)
ISBN: 978-1-4908-2168-9 (sc)
ISBN: 978-1-4908-2169-6 (hc)

Library of Congress Control Number: 2014901447

Printed in the United States of America.

WestBow Press rev. date: 3/7/2014

Dedicated to
Irish
She celebrated Christmas
With the King of Kings,
Jesus Christ
2013

CONTENTS

ACKNOWLEDGMENTS

I would like to thank those who have helped me with their encouragement, expertise in their field of work and kindness of their time:

My elder son Richard who has given of so many hours of his knowledge in editing, editing, editing during the several years of my thinking then planning and finally writing this story. Richard I couldn't have gotten it all together with out your help. Thank you.

Thank you my daughter, Nancy, for your encouragement, "Mom this idea you have of some fictitious Christian Characters would be a good story. You need to write this story." Thank you, Nancy Girl.

Paulette, I appreciate the hours you spent, while recovering from the surgery on your neck (spine), smoothing out and clarifying sentences and paragraphs, showing your gift as an excellent School Teacher. Thank you, Polly girl.

Second Son, Chuck, though you are too far away to help with the book, I want to acknowledge your willing and generous heart that is always there to help when someone is in need. That is admirable, dear son..

Thank you dear Granddaughter, Kim, for your Nursing advice and suggestions in the part where the Character, Jill, falls in the old cistern and is hospitalized. Thank you Sweetheart.

Grandson Rick Rector and friend Brian Putnam, two fellows who put their lives on the line as Officers of the Law, thank you for direction and advice in parts of the book concerning Police work. Thank you both.

Thanks to you, my dear friend Helen, for putting in your time reading and finding missed errors and skips in the book. I just know those errors are the fault of my contrary mac computer. Thank you for your time. I appreciate you.

CHAPTER 1

Jack as a child

Jack was a precocious child with a giant imagination. You wouldn't say he was bad or obnoxious. He just had an active mind and was very inquisitive.

Sitting on the floor in the living room playing with his Action Figures he heard his mom call, "Jack, get your hands washed, for dinner."

Then Shiny Man, standing beside him said, "Obey your mother, Jack."

Jack thought, "Why did she have to call me now? The Philistines were winning the war and killing all the good people." God was not going to like that.

Jack was captivating, warm hearted and friendly. You didn't have to be around him long before you felt like, "Yeah, life's good!" The little guy started rubbing off on you. He was endearing and he had a giant imagination. Though only four years old he had confidence about himself, an inquisitive mind and sureness about knowledge, which he had gathered. You could see how he paid close attention to people's conversations. He was anxious, but not obnoxious, about contributing to the conversation and learning what other's opinions were. Jack was a pretty sharp little fellow.

This endearing fellow would have liked to have a little more to say about the things he had to do; particularly concerning when he should eat, when he should go to bed, and especially why he should put his toys away. Some things didn't make sense to young Jack.

As with a lot of us, one of the very most important things in his young life was food. But about the food—well, some of the times he was not hungry but had to go to the table and eat anyway. Then again, sometimes he was hungry, but he had to tell his stomach to wait because his mom told him it was not time to eat. Where was the reasoning in that? Jack remembered his mother told him he must be patient. He had asked dad what the word patient meant and his dad told him, "A patient is what you are when you go to the doctor," but he didn't need to go to a doctor.

Jack thought it might be a good idea to just put food in a safe place, (away from germs, of course) where it was easy to get to. Then people could eat when they wanted, what they wanted, where they wanted and especially, as much as they wanted. Then eating would be fun.

Now the toy thing was a very serious subject—and his mom said a *subject* was something you are talking about. What he was talking about were the times he got all his toys just the way he wanted them, which took a lot of work and only then, when he had played with them for just a little while he had to put them away. His mom said she couldn't help him with that problem; she wasn't much help there.

Next there was the bed thing: why couldn't he just simply lie down where he was when he felt sleepy? Was it always necessary to take a bath and put on pajamas? Also, it seemed to Jack, like such a waste of time to sleep when he wasn't tired, so why must a guy have to go to bed when there was so much to do?

His mom told him, "Sometimes we are tired but just don't know it until we get in bed and snuggled down." Jack did like to snuggle under his new, warm and soft, Super Man blanket.

His dad told him how to take care of it all. He said, "Just let it go, Son, just roll with the wave and don't worry, just go with the flow." Jack decided he would let that go because he sure didn't want water waving and rolling in his bed--he decided to let it go.

"Grandma, Grandma," shouted Jack and he leaped to his feet and ran to take Grandma's hand as she entered the living room. He was happy when she came to visit him and his family because she would often play with him. She didn't seem to go about doing things that seemed to be a waste of time. His mom vacuumed so many times he wondered if the floor might go up in the vacuum cleaner.

"Come sit with me, Grandma!" He was playing with his action figures on the living room floor. He was playing near the fireplace where the slate floor was smooth.

"Where is Grandpa?" he asked, as she settled next him, with a couple of grunts. He wondered why old people made noises when they sat down and especially when they stood up.

"Grandpa is at work." she replied as she gave him a little hug. "He will come later. Do you miss him?"

"Yes, but it's okay."

His grandfather was a wise man, just like his dad. He would often agree with Jack as they talked things over, but then Grandpa, a lot of the time, would say words Jack didn't understand completely, Jack would have to decide if he wanted to ask him to explain but didn't want still more words he couldn't understand. There too, he would just let whatever Grandpa was saying go without too many questions. Grandpa seemed to like those big words like compo si--and some more letters. He would have to look it up in his dictionary. Then, when he looked in the dictionary, there were sometimes more words he didn't understand.

He did like the word compounding. That was easy, it meant to come and be pounding. His dad bought him a hammer that fit his hand. His dad showed him how his big hammer fit his big hand.

When Jack held his dad's hammer it didn't fit his hand like it did his dad's hand. He was anxious for his hand to grow big enough to fit his dad's hammer.

As Grandma came and sat down by where Jack was playing with his action figures she pointed to one of them and asked, "What is the name of this fellow, Jack?"

After telling her the name of the action figure, he went on arranging them. Grandma repeated the name he had said.

He turned to her with a rather stern look, studied her for a moment, and said, "No, look at me, Grandma." He took hold of her chin, as his mother had done with him, to get her to look straight at him. "Look at me, Grandma, real close. His name is Dar-th Va-der. Can you say that?"

Rather amazed at the clear diction of such a young child, she repeated after him: "Dar-th Va-der."

Shiny Man cautioned Jack, softly saying, "Remember to be respectful, Jack."

Jack said, 'I'm sorry Shiny Man."

To show he was pleased at Grandma's success, Jack kindly praised her. "That's correct, Grandma. You did very well. Now, can you say Darth Vader?" Again, he praised her when she said it right. Jack got up to his knees, and putting an arm around her neck, gave her a soft, damp, kiss on the check. He grinned at her and sat back down.

His grandmother remembered how she used to take her daughter's chin, Jack's mother, in her hand for the very same reason, to get her attention. It amused and pleased her that her daughter had done the same with her little boy. She was startled but found it was working. Grandma was very sure she would never forget that action figure's name.

His mother then, musically, called to him. "Jack, get your hands washed for supper."

Grandma raised her eyebrows in a friendly way, smiled at Jack, stood up, with a couple more grunts, and went to the kitchen to help her daughter.

With her face showing amazement, she said, "Lisa, that child talks like an adult." Hearing that, Jack was sure it must be a good thing.

Jack's mom was busy with getting their dinner on the table; she smiled and said, "You know, its amazing now that I think of it, ever since he fell in the pool his vocabulary has markedly increased.

In order to encourage Jack, his mom repeated her request; "Get your hands washed for supper, sweetheart." In a more stern voice she added, "Do it now, Son."

Jack quietly said to himself, "Oh, my, not right now! I have to save the good people from the Philistines."

Shiny Man, standing beside Jack, reminded him, "Obey, your mother, Jack, remember, what we talked about."

Jack looked up at Shiny Man, pouting just a bit. "I wish you would be really helpful so I could have more fun." Then he called out, "Coming, Mom." He headed for the bathroom.

Shiny Man smiled and went with him.

Grandma came from the kitchen and suggested they wash their hands together. Always the little helper, Jack thought that was a good idea.

"Grandma, that's an excellent idea because then I can show you the new thing I have learned."

Jack remembered Shiny Man's instruction, he was to be kind so, he smiled at Grandma and took her hand while they walked into the bathroom.

As they shared the sink, Jack held his hand out and said, "Mom says I should put soap on my hand about as big as my thumbnail like this, and then with water, make suds, sing Happy Birthday two times and then rinse the soap off--she said that is how long it takes to kill the dangerous germs on our hands." He sang Happy Birthday two times and rinsed his hands.

"Now you do it, Grandma, and sing two times." Grandma was a willing student feeling pride and a grandmother's love for her second grandson. She followed instructions *and* sang Happy Birthday twice. With a big smile that spread over his whole body—and face—and a generous spirit Jack shared the towel with Grandma as they dried their hands.

"You're lots of fun, Grandma," said Jack as he snuggled and smiled up at her.

She put her hand on his little shoulders and looking down at him, studied his sweet face. He was no longer a toddler. His face was changing into that of an older child. He had a hint of freckles across his pert little nose. The baby curls were gone and his hair was getting thicker and darker; he had a big boy haircut. She was sure he was going to be a very handsome man.

"Thank you, my sweet grandson. You are fun too," Grandma told Jack as she gave him another little hug. Off to the dining room they went, holding hands. Shiny Man took Jack's other hand.

Jack drew in his breath sharply, "Oh, I should have introduced you to Shiny Man, Grandma. I'm sorry. I forgot." Jack had a warm, friendly feeling for Shiny Man. He turned to Shiny Man and said, " This is my Grandma, Shiny Man." Grandma looked where Jack was looking and smiled with her lips closed. Jack could tell she liked Shiny Man too.

Then he remembered he was supposed to thank God for things, so he said under his breath, "Thank you, God, for Shiny Man. He is really neat. Maybe I should have washed my face too. Oh yes, and thank you for my Grandma."

When they were alone after eating, Grandma asked Lisa, Jack's mom, if she knew Jack talked about someone called Shiny Man.

"Who is that?" Grandma asked.

"Oh, that is Jack's imaginary friend," answered Jack's mom.

Grandma could see that Jack's mom was not anxious to talk about it, for she looked at her husband and rather quickly changed the subject. Grandma wondered if there was some irritation with that. Children often had make-believe friends and that was fine, she thought, but was not about to comment on it. She went on talking about Janet's excellent dinner and her recipes.

CHAPTER 2

Faith of a child

Jack had a brother whom he admired. His name was Todd and was about ten years older than Jack. Todd was hired to cut their neighbor's grass on his small, front lawn and the neighbor agreed to pay Todd ten dollars. When Todd was finished the man said to him, "Todd will you take some change?"

"Sure, Mr. Greer, that will be fine and thanks." was Todd's reply. Mr. Greer gave him a five-dollar bill and four one-dollar bills along with the change—there were mostly dimes. Mr. Greer told Todd thanks for cutting the small front lawn and they shook hands. Mr. Greer did not look too well. "Are you alright, Sir?

"Well, I think I have lifted too many heavy things and my back is pretty tired. That's why I asked you to cut my front lawn. I'll be fine when I rest; thanks for asking, Jack.

"You're welcome and anytime, Sir."

When Todd got home he laid the money out on the table, happy to have made some money, especially when it was so easy and didn't take much time. Todd's little brother, Jack was standing by Todd and was in awe of all that money his big brother had earned.

Todd turned to his little brother. "Jack, it sure helped when you brought me that glass of ice cold lemonade when I was halfway through. The hot sun was making me sweat and uncomfortable. I want to thank you, little brother, and I want to give you all these dimes for helping me."

Todd's mom had another glass of lemonade for him, and he thanked her as he took it. She turned to ask Jack if he wanted some but he had disappeared. In a moment, Jack came back to the kitchen but he had a very sad face.

"Why do you look so sad, Jack?" his mother asked.

Jack stood with head down, drooped shoulders and turned down mouth said, "I don't want dimes, I want dollars like Todd."

Todd and his mother stared at one another with wide opened eyes. "This little guy is smart!" whispered Todd to his mother as they both had to hide smiles.

Turning to Jack he held one of the dollars in his hand. "Would you trade the dimes for this dollar, Jack?"

Jack's face broke out into a wide grin, "Yes! Thanks Todd." He took the dollar and skipped into his room to put it in his bank. When he came back he was all smiles, and he told Todd and his mom, "I remember some man at the grocery store said, "I will take the dollars anytime over the change,' so that's why I wanted the dollar—not the dimes."

Jack didn't understand just what the man meant but was sure the man was wise—like his dad and grandpa. He knew they both didn't want to carry *a lot* of change in their pockets, and he knew they would rather have dollars. Jack wanted dollars, not dimes.

Jack started school and of all the kids that he got to know, there was a girl named Jill, and she was his favorite. He met her the first day of kindergarten, and fell in love with her when she punched out another kindergartener that had pulled her pigtail. With one quick whack, she surprised him and flattened him. He lay on the ground with surprise in his eyes, afraid to get up.

Jack well remembered the details of that incident. Jill was dressed all in pink and ribbons and standing with clenched fists and angry eyes. This was a gal not to be reckoned with. When Jack tried to hide his smile, she looked at him with narrowed eyes. She tightened her mouth, and stuck out her chin. Jack thought he might be next to hit the ground. Instead, Jill turned and ran over to her friends at the swings. All this having come from such a tiny girl startled Jack. She was even shorter than him.

At snack time, Jack braved the chance and sat down by Jill, though not too close. When she kept eating, he gave her one of his pretzels. She held out a grape without looking at Jack and put the pretzel in her mouth. They became best friends. When Jack got off the bus at his house after school he felt so happy. He knew he was going to marry her.

At suppertime, Jack had a lot on his mind, so he didn't talk as much as usual. Deep in thought, he realized that growing up and going to school sure made things different in a person's life. Breaking in on his thoughts, his mother asked him, "What's on your mind, Jack?" He was glad she asked because he liked talking about Jill.

"Well, there's this girl at school in my grade, and I think I will marry her. But I know that I have to ask her dad to see if it is all right with him. I learned about that on TV."

Jack's mom, with her glass in her hand, looked at him for a moment, holding the drink she had taken into her mouth. She suddenly chuckled, then choked, and water came out of her nose and mouth and went all over the table. Jack's older brother burst out laughing. Dad gave him one of those looks, that lets you know you have done something you shouldn't have. Jack knew his brother shouldn't have laughed at Mom. Dad had a half-smile on one side of his face, but he kept on eating. Jack's brother couldn't hold it in--he jumped up, excused himself, and went into the other room, where he roared with laughter.

Dad remembered what Jack had told them and said, "We'll have to talk about that after supper, okay, Son?"

"Sure Dad. You're not going to punish Todd, are you? It was kinda funny when Mom spit water all over the table!" His dad, struggling to be serious, shook his head, no, and kept eating.

Todd came back to the table and apologized, he said he was sorry for laughing. Then, smiling at Jack, he playfully messed Jack's hair with his hand. "You're quite a kick, little brother."

Jack didn't know what that meant, as he hadn't kicked anybody. Jack reached up and gave Todd a soft brother punch on his arm then ate some more of his corn.

Jack remembered his dad said they would talk it over—his mom spitting water all over the table. His dad was pretty smart and Jack liked it when Dad and he talked things over. They usually went into Dad's office or out on the front porch. Sometimes they'd go for a walk together and talk guy stuff. This time they went for a walk. His dad wondered if he should forget about Jack talking about marriage at his age.

They didn't need a sweater for it was a nice warm evening, as most of South Carolina evenings are in late August, and it was pleasant to walk in their neighborhood. The yards and shrubs were neatly trimmed. Flowers were plentiful, with many different varieties. Jack didn't know all the names of them but he thought they were sure pretty. Big beautiful roses were especially showy. That name he did know for they had some in their yard. Most of the houses in his neighborhood were fairly large and attractive. Some were two-story and some were one-story and spread out. Jack liked the spread out ones; they were like his house.

Jack skipped and danced along picking up interesting things to examine then drop if it didn't look like something he could put in his ever-growing special collection.

He petted the neighbor's dog that ran out to greet them. After a few strokes on the dog's back Jack pointed his finger at him and commanded, "Sit." Jack had heard the neighbor man who owned the dog tell him that. The dog sat back on his haunches. That surprised Jack when the dog obeyed him. Feeling good about that success he repeated the command with the pointed finger. The dog lied down and put his head between his paws and his perky ears went down. That surprised Jack even more. He turned to tell his dad about that amazing word that the dog understood, but his dad had walked on so Jack ran to catch up with him.

When they turned left at the corner Jack gave a couple happy little jumps because he knew where they were going.

There was a park two blocks from their house that had lots of fun things to see and do. Entering the park they walked past a large bandstand where different bands played for the public some summer evenings. Jack knew that because he and his mom and dad would go to listen sometimes. Todd didn't care much about it so didn't go with them. They had to take folding chairs with them. Jack often got tired of sitting but his mom was nice. She brought a little snack for him; usually small pieces of candy, but they were wrapped and took quite a while to unwrap each one. It was okay though. He most of the time got all of them unwrapped and eaten before it was time for them to go home. If there were any left he would take them home and put them in his bedroom where he had a candy-jar on his dresser.

Still walking along with his dad, there was a long building, open on all sides, with tables where people could have family picnics. Further on they came to what Jack especially liked.

"I like this the best of everything in the park, Dad"

"You know what, Jack? I like this the best too."

There was a water fountain with water shooting up in the air and coming down into the fountain. The water wasn't deep, but there were lots of big fish in it. If someone brought bread or something with them they could feed the fish. It was fun to see the fish zip up to the top of the water and snatch the pieces of food. Then they would dart back down. Jack and his dad hadn't brought any bread with them that time.

Jack's dad took hold of Jack's hand and they walked on. He thought, "How am I going to tell Jack about deciding whom a fellow was going to marry? I guess I better talk to him again about that make believe friend he keeps talking about." Jack's dad had a strained look on his face

Jack loved his dad and he knew his dad loved him. Shiny Man took his other hand. Jack thought he had better ask for permission though, so he wouldn't get in trouble; he wanted to say it nicely, "It's all right if Shiny Man comes along, isn't it Dad?"

His dad stopped walking, dropped Jack's hand, turned, put his hands on his hips, and looked down at Jack with a frown.

"Jack, I have told you that you are old enough to stop this talk about make-believe people." He turned and started back for their house. Jack was glad Dad hadn't yelled at him. His dad didn't do much yelling.

Jack felt better, though, as he followed his dad home. He thought he would talk to his mom about his dad not liking Shiny Man. Then he felt kind of bad again and said to Shiny Man, "I'm sorry Dad doesn't want me to talk to you."

Shiny Man smiled down at Jack and put his hand on his little shoulder very gently. "I understand how he feels, Jack, and it's all right"

That made Jack feel much better, he didn't want to hurt Shiny Man's feelings. "Thank you," he said with a smile on his little face. He knew he was going to have to talk to his mom about his dad not liking Shiny Man.

Jack's dad felt bad for scolding his small son. He couldn't figure out why it riled him so when Jack talked about that bothersome make believe person.

When Jack said his prayers that night, he told God he was sorry if he had accidently kicked someone that day, and then he thanked Him. Jack's Mom had told him we are supposed to say thanks for all things. She showed him the place in his Bible. "See, here it is in Ephesians 5:20.

She explained to Jack. She said, "God doesn't do bad things. He may stop some bad thing or He may not. If He doesn't stop a bad thing it's because He had a good purpose for not stopping it. So we can thank Him, knowing, He *can,* stop a bad thing, or not and if He doesn't stop a bad thing we can thank Him for the good reason that He has in mind, for not stopping it. He never makes a mistake. He loves us."

In spite of all that puzzling explanation, Jack still didn't feel like thanking God for *all* things, but he did say thanks anyway—Jack knew he wasn't as smart as his mom or God.

Then he remembered something. "By the way, God," he said, "I found out that Jill's name is Jill, and that is really cool, because, you know, Jack and Jill went up the hill. Oh, and thanks that Mom wanted me to tell her about Shiny Man sometime. I like Shiny Man, God. Thanks."

He got up from his knees and snuggled under his new Superman blanket. He felt like he was going to go to sleep—his mom was right—about the bed thing. He went to sleep."

CHAPTER 3

A Party and Near Tragedy

The next day at school, when Jack told Jill he was going to marry her, he didn't get down on one knee because he thought he was too young for that. Jill put her hand over her mouth and just giggled. Jack took that as an okay. He thought girls were so silly most of the time, but it was okay, because he knew Jill would get over that as she got older. Jack's mom didn't giggle. Jack sort of liked Jill's giggle, though. It made him want to laugh too.

Going to school was one of his favorite things because he got to see all the kids there. He liked seeing Jill the best, since she always played with him the most. Jack liked to swing on the bars, and she did too. Sometimes they would trade snacks.

Jack didn't know Jill lived only two blocks from him until she had a birthday party and invited him.

"Mom, I know just the best present for Jill. I will give her an engagement ring for her present." His Mom had to turn away and wipe off the counter top—again.

"How do I handle this?" she muttered under her breath. Turning to Jack she said, "I don't think that would be a very good idea, Sweetheart."

"Why not mom?" Jack asked, void of all understanding. That didn't make sense to him, but he knew he should be respectful. Shiny Man had told him about that.

"For one thing, Jack, girls usually get engagement rings after high school or even after college. Another thing, her finger grows and would not fit her in a very short time; mostly because it is too soon, so after high--."

"Oh, I see, Mom," said Jack, trying to hide his sadness, he didn't want any more explanation, "I'll wait." That was going to be an awfully long time. He just knew he would have a hard time explaining it to Jill.

He was disappointed but instead he chose to give her a big box of supplies for blowing huge colored bubbles. They all got to blow the bubbles at her party. He thought Jill took the sad news, about no ring, pretty good. She just looked serious at him, tipped her head with a bit of a frown, and then smiled and thanked him for the bubble-kit.

After he got home from the party, Jack found that his mom and Todd were baking cookies. He was full of all the goodies at Jill's party but, that was okay, he sat on a stool eating his mom and Todd's cookies; his mom sat down and had a couple of cookies with him. He told her Jill was okay about the ring then thought it was a good time to also tell his mom about his other problem.

"Mom, Dad doesn't want me to talk to Shiny Man anymore. I really like him," he confided. He felt his chin start to quiver, so he tried hard not to cry.

His mom smiled a little, put her head to one side and tenderly put her hand under his tiny chin and asked, "Jack, do you remember the first time you ever saw Shiny Man?"

"Oh, sure, it was when I was at the bottom of the swimming pool."

Jack didn't notice that his mother's smile disappeared and her eyes opened wide as her cookie froze halfway to her open mouth. "Oh!" she said, unbelieving, and quickly put the whole cookie in her mouth. Jack's mom was sure then that Jack had had a hallucination when he was drowning.

"Are you saving the cookies for supper, Mom?"

With a forced smile, she said, "I think we may have one more. Your father will be a little late coming home."

Not wanting to let this conversation end, she asked, "How did you get through the gate, Sweetheart? Remember, you were such a little boy, and we had a weight that held the gate closed."

"Sure, I remember, Mom. When Todd's friends came to swim and it was time for them to go home, Todd's friend Jeff put the weight up on the post so the gate would stay open. He had a lot of things he had to pick up and take home with him. I know we used to say, 'Remember to put the wait, on the gate.' Why did we have to wait on the gate, Mom?"

Amused but in awe of what her son was remembering, Jack's mom told him the difference between the words "wait" and "weight." Jack knew he would have to look up those two words in the dictionary his grandpa had given him for Christmas. His mom thought for a moment and said, "So you just walked in. Did you want to swim?"

"No, Mom, not without you or Dad there. I just tried to get the weight off of the post where Jeff put it. He put it there so the gate would stay open so he could get all of his stuff out to their car. I knew though, that the weight was not supposed to be up there."

Jack looked out the kitchen window as he was remembering. "It was so heavy it made me stumble backward, and I went into the pool and went to the bottom. I couldn't breathe, and I was so scared for a while, but a shiny man came through the water and helped me not to be scared. He held my hand. He's nice, Mom. But it was okay, 'cause Dad got my body out, huh, Mom?"

It all came back to Jack's mom—that frightful afternoon. She, Todd, and Len, Jack's dad, were telling Todd's friends good-bye.

Jeff called to them as they drove away, saying, "Tell Jack good-bye. He's a neat little guy."

They turned to look for their three-year-old, but Jack was not there.

"Oh no," came Todd's strangled cry, and he started running for the backyard with Jack's mom and dad right on his heels. He remembered Jeff telling him he hadn't closed the gate. Fear paralyzed them as they reached the pool's edge. Jack was on the very bottom, not moving. Jack's dad was in the pool in an instant and came up holding his son's limp body. Todd helped him out as he reached the edge of the pool, with Jack in his arms.

Kicking chairs out of the way, Len shouted, "Call 911--hurry." Laying his boy on the sidewalk he started CPR. As he systematically worked on Jack, he was calling on God, for His help; thanking Him that he had worked as a lifeguard, and knew what to do.

Their mom raced to the outside phone and called 911, "Hurry, hurry, my little boy—my little--son has fallen in the pool and drowned!" She could hardly talk or make sense as the person wanted her to stay on the phone. They wanted her to stay on the phone answering questions. Tears were flowing so fast and her throat was closing up...!

Todd ran for the house crying and pleading with God, "God save my little brother, please don't let him die—forgive me for not closing the gate right a way, I'm so sorry, God,"

He dashed into the house, thanking God that his dad had been teaching him how to drive. He grabbed the car keys off the hook by the kitchen door, ran into the garage, banged on the pad that opened the garage door and pulled the car out onto the driveway. He could hear sirens in the distance so he pulled the car back into the garage a ways. Turning the motor off, he jumped out of the car, he raced to the curb waving frantically, to direct the fire truck and ambulance into the driveway; help had arrived.

Jack opened his eyes and weakly said, "Where's the shiny man?" Not taking time to answer that strange question, Len struggled to his feet, picked up his son to rush him to the emergency room but stood just in time to thrust Jack into the reaching arms of the paramedic. Seeing the child was conscious, the paramedic lost no time in getting Jack into the ambulance for observation and to stabilize the small patient. It was only a matter of a few minutes and the ambulance was speeding on the way to the hospital with siren blasting the neighborhood.

As the ambulance left the driveway, Len grabbed the hand of Jack's mom and they were in the car as Todd jumped into the back seat. Only blocks behind the ambulance, they reached the emergency entrance in time to see Jack being rolled into the hospital for the help that was waiting for him.

Parking the car and turning off the key, Len grabbed his wife and son's hand to pray. They sat together to pray, giving thanks to the Lord for saving Jack, for getting them to him in time. They gave thanks for the warning given them by Todd's friend as he called his message about Jack while they drove away, Len prayed "Thank You Lord, that Your hand is not too short to save." (Isaiah 59:1; Behold, the Lord's hand is not shortened, that it cannot save; neither His ear heavy, that it cannot hear.) With a grateful heart and somewhat calmer, they went into the hospital to see about Jack.

Sitting with his mom as they talked and ate cookies, Jack looked quizzically at her. Words began to pour out of his mouth, "I couldn't stop falling, Mom. I guess I was too little, but then a shiny man came through the water and held my hand, and then I wasn't scared. (Mat 18:10 "Jesus called a little child unto Him...their Angels in heaven do always behold the face my Father...)

"We watched Dad get my body off the bottom of the pool; Todd helped him out. Dad laid my body down on the sidewalk. I don't think Dad saw Shiny Man, 'cause he was too busy taking my body out of the pool, and Todd helped Dad get out of the pool. Then I got out of the pool and went back into my body, and Shiny Man went away. Then we went to the hospital, and I was all right. I don't think Shiny Man went to the hospital with us, 'cause I don't think Dad likes Shiny Man very much. He doesn't want me to talk to him." Jack took a deep constrained breath.

"I see," uttered Jack's mom as she put her arm around her small son's shoulders. She took another cookie and gave Jack another one as well.

Jack looked up at his mom, and he took it with a terrific smile saying, "Gee, thanks, Mom, you're great."

"You're welcome, honey. We are so thankful to the Lord you were saved. You were so very brave."

Jack didn't know how he had been brave, but he didn't want to ask her to explain how he did that.

Pushing the horrific vision from her mind, Jack's mom stuffed another whole cookie in her mouth so she wouldn't cry about what seemed like nothing to Jack. She tried to smile at her precious son as a band of gratitude wrapped around her soul.

The mystery of how Jack had even gotten into the pool area was finally been solved. Jack's mom again gratefully offered thanks to the Lord for Jack's safe rescue. As she wondered about the young child's amazing story, she knew she would have to talk to her husband about Jack's unusual imagination.

C H A P T E R   4

Tween and Teen Years

One day Jill called Jack on the phone; he was so surprised. She told him that he and his mom were invited to come to her house for cookies and tea. He wondered how she knew that his mom liked tea. "Can we go, Mom?"

"Of course, Sweetheart. Tell her we'd love to and thank her. Ask her when and what time."

Jack's mom and Jill's mom became best friends, and before they knew it, their families were going to the same church. Jack saw Shiny Man more often then. When Shiny Man was with him, Jack felt real close to God. He was sorry the other kids didn't see him too.

As soon as he and Jill were old enough, they became a part of the youth group at their church. Jack liked it because he got to be with Jill and the other kids more. When he couldn't think of something to say to new kids, Jill always filled in the awkward minutes. That was cool.

One time a couple of new kids were visiting and wanted to go outdoors. They wanted him to go out too. Jack told them, "Naw, I think we are all supposed to stay together inside."

Jack didn't want to leave Shiny Man either, even if no one else saw him, so he didn't go out. He stayed with Jill and the rest of the group and Shiny Man. Later he heard that there was some kind of trouble outdoors with the visiting kids. He was glad that he hadn't wanted to go out.

All through grade school and high school, Jill was a tomboy and a touch-me-not person but could beat Jack at lots of things. He just wished she wouldn't beat him in most everything. He wondered if she cheated sometimes, but he figured she didn't and that she was just very good at certain things. Jill got to be taller than him. Jack really hated it that he was short and skinny. Even so, he got to be on the football team in sixth grade.

Because he was small for his age, the other guys on the team knocked him around a lot. They liked him and weren't mean, but they called him a lot of names, like Short Stuff, Pee Wee, and Little Guy. Sometimes it riled him, but it felt good just to be able to wear the thick pads and other football equipment. He even liked to go to practice. When the plays would get pretty rough he stayed on the outer edges. All the guys were just bigger than him.

Students were required to have a physical to be on the team. While Jack and his mom were at the doctor's office, Jack asked him, "Gee, Doctor, can't you give me something to make me bigger?"

The doctor stopped writing and looked at Jack in a friendly way. He stared at the floor for a moment with understanding and said, "You know, Jack, you may not believe it, but I was just like you," he looked up and added, " clear up to when I started high school."

"Yeah, that is hard to believe. You must weigh over two hundred pounds." The doctor was over six feet tall and had large muscles.

"No," he said, "I weigh one hundred and sixty-seven." Jack felt a whole lot better. The doctor went on. "Considering the size of your hands and feet, I'd judge you'll be a pretty good-sized fellow by the time you stop growing."

Jack felt like giving the doctor a hug, but instead they shared a fist bump. The doctor gave Jack an easy punch in the arm, and Jack gave him the same back. Jack couldn't wait for his next year's physical. He wasn't sure, but it looked like there were some tears in Mom's eyes. She smiled softly at Jack. He thought his mom was cool.

Wouldn't you know it--Jill grew taller, though she was skinny like him. She was a girl, but she could really bat. Once, when the shortstop on Jack's team was sick and couldn't play, the fellows let Jill play on their neighborhood team. She fixed her hair in her cap so no one on the team they played against would know she was a girl. She batted in four runs. She could sure lay that ball out there. Jack batted in one run, and they won nine to four.

Jack could make macaroni and cheese better than Jill. They usually made it at Jack's house. Jack's was soft and gooey; he added extra cheese, but he didn't tell her that.

Jill was faster, though, and his Mom said, "I can't figure out how Jill never makes quite as much mess, Jack." He knew she was teasing, but somehow, Jack always felt intimidated by Jill, he still knew he was going to marry her someday.

However, when it came to school, Jack got As in math, while Jill got As in English; one time he only got a B+. Jack wondered why in the world it was so important to know how to conjugate a verb or how to diagram a sentence. Jill sometimes helped Jack with English assignments, but she wouldn't let him help her with math homework. He couldn't figure *that* out.

One time while he was in seventh grade, Jack was walking home alone from practice and three big tough guys from the other side of town were pushing him around. They backed him up against a fence. One of them took his bat, and another took his glove and acted smart. They wouldn't give them back to him.

About that time, Jill came riding along. When she saw what was going on, she got off her bike, laid it on the ground, took a gallon jug of milk out of her bike's basket, and walked right into the middle of those boys and started smashing the big bullies in the head with the milk jug one at a time before they realized what had hit them. Jill was a little taller than those boys. If they tried to say something she would hit them again. Their eyes were so big that Jack thought they might pop right out of their heads. They dropped Jack's bat and glove and started backing away, acting like they were laughing.

"Where did that hellcat come from?" Jack heard one of them say, as a switchblade fell out of one of their pockets, and they ran away, fast.

Jill put the jug of milk back in her bike's basket and picked up her bike. "Sorry bunch of heathens," she said as she pedaled on down the street toward her house. Jack thought those guys had better watch it, talking so carelessly about hell.

He just looked at the knife. He wanted nothing to do with it and was thinking, "They will probably come back for that when I leave. Jack, did not dally, he went home

Jill's mom never had Jill's hair cut short, and Jack was glad of that. Her pigtails had grown pretty long by the time they were in ninth grade. She came to school with her pigtails combed out one day, and Jack could see why she almost always had pigtails; her dark brown hair was wavy, and Jill told him it was hard to do anything with. Jack thought her hair was pretty but he was sure glad he wasn't a girl. He wondered how she washed all of it.

During their junior year of high school, their youth group had a swimming party at the town swimming pool. That was the first time that Jack noticed Jill had some nice curves. He hated that the other guys noticed too! A couple of them whistled at her. She acted like she didn't like it, so Jack didn't whistle. He went over and sort of stood by her.

She walked a little closer to him and said, "Beat you to the diving tower," then jumped into the water and he followed her. They had fun dunking one another. She could sure hold her breath a long time.

Jack and Jill ran around with the same group, swimming, riding bikes, and playing beach volleyball together, even if they didn't live close to the beach. A lot of their friend's families even went to the same church, so most of them were in the same youth group. In the summer, some of the guys took on different handyman-type jobs. Jill's mom was teaching her to sew. The dresses, shorts, and skirts she made were as nice as the ones in stores. Jack liked it when she started learning to cook, because he was often her taster. Brownies were Jack's favorite of all the things she made. Jill would give him something to taste then turn her back but watched his face over her shoulder when he tasted what she had made. She tightened her mouth until he remarked about how the food tasted.

He had presence of mind to say, "I don't know how, but everything you make tastes so good."

Jill would then walk away to the stove with a pleased look. Her mother had to turn her back so they wouldn't see her smile. Jill would then give him an extra brownie when he left to go home. He knew he was going to marry her.

C H A P T E R   5

Getting Ready For The Prom

During their senior year, there was the senior prom to look forward to. That special occasion caused a lot of the seniors to start pairing off—that is, those who hadn't already done so. Jack sort of wanted Jill to say he was her boyfriend, but he didn't tell her that. If he'd hint at it, she would pretend to be disinterested so he'd drop it. He guessed that was one of the problems with treating a girl like one of the guys. Since they found themselves on a couple of the prom committees helping to prepare for the occasion, it seemed like they really should go, like it or not. Jack heard another guy ask Jill to go to the prom with him. He thought for sure by the look on Jill's face that she was going to punch him. Instead, she just shoved him away. "Okay, so I was just kidding–okay?" the guy's face turned red. Jack wanted to go to the Prom, and take Jill, but if he asked her and she did the same to him, he wondered how he'd feel? Jack was very cautious perhaps feeling it best not to invite trouble.

When they were on their way home from school one day, Jack finally got the courage to casually say they should go together. Jill acted like she was mad. She blushed fiercely, and with great difficulty snapped at him, "Well, my mom made a special dress for it and I thought about telling Jacob I had changed my mind and that I would go with *him*."

Jack thought for a moment that Jill really was going to push him down, instead she tossed her head, turned, and walked briskly away with clenched fist and stiff, straight back, towards her house, as fast as she could go. He usually walked to her house with her, sometimes going in with her, but knew he better not follow her that day. Because Jack lived only a couple of blocks from her, he decided he would wait to call her until he got in his room. He guessed he had waited pretty long to suggest going together—it was the day before the prom. He couldn't figure out why it had been so hard for him to ask her.

Jack didn't want to talk to anyone when he got in the house, so he went right to his room to call Jill to figure things out. His cell phone rang, and he saw Jill was calling. He didn't say hello; he just started to blubber. "I'm sorry Jill, I'm sorry, I really want you to go with me." When she didn't say anything, he thought she had hung up. "Jill?"

Jill snickered. "You just better wear a tux," she said. *Then* she hung up.

Jack didn't know very much about the word euphoria, but he was positive that was what was making his heart thump in his ears and tap dance in his chest. Prom was going to be their first real date. If he had hinted to Jill about their going out, Jill always changed the subject. Yet they always seemed to be together—like since kindergarten. Where he went, Jill would go too. If she wanted to go somewhere, somehow they ended up going together—yet not actually dating. They were somehow, simply, best friends.

Now that they were actually going to have a date he wanted to go and do something great, like maybe washing the supper dishes for his mom. Instead he decided he would clean his room. When he opened his closet door to hang up his clothes, he found a tux hanging there in front of him. He almost shouted to himself, "Man, what great parents

I have. I would have been sunk if they hadn't gone ahead and gotten it for me. Tomorrow would have probably been too late to get one."

At supper that evening he told his mom and dad that he saw the tux and thanked them. His dad asked him if it fit. "Yeah, it fits perfect, thanks, and Jill said her mother made her a dress for the prom." He couldn't look into his parent's minds, which were saying, "Yeah, we know." He had taken driver's Ed and passed with flying colors, so his dad said he could take the family car. Jack was ecstatic.

Jack and Jill had no knowledge that both their parents were never pushing, yet always subtly helping things along in subtle ways.

His mom asked him if he liked to dance, and Jack said, "No, but Jill won't want to dance."

"Well, what if she wants to?" she persisted.

"Well, I guess I'll have to tell one of my friends to ask her to dance."

His dad joined the conversation, "Your mom and I used to go to dances. I sure wouldn't have wanted other guys to dance with her— well, maybe a couple of dances--maybe. Your mom was fantastic. She worked at a dance studio, before we got married and taught people to dance."

"Dad, are you kidding? Mom, would you show me how, just a little bit?" Happy that the news worked, his mom taught him some basic slow steps and some fast ones that would get him by, like showing him to twirl Jill. Jack declared, man, am I ever glad for this!" He figured that would help him score points with Jill on their date. He didn't want to make a fool of himself.

He had seen dancing on T.V. but secretly wondered if Jill would knock him out if he put his arm around her if they danced some slow dances. She was never much into touching and could whither him with just a look. It reminded him of one time they were laughing about something and he put his hand on her shoulder. She stiffened, looked at his hand then bored a hole through him with her steely eyes. He removed his hand--he hadn't meant anything by it. She became fun Jill again.

His dad suggested he ought to just casually offer his arm to Jill if they had to go down stairs, because she might have high heels on." He was willing but he still wondered. He would just wait and see. Another thing he saw guys do was open the car door for their date, to get in or get out. Jill usually jumped out when they were in someone's car and got where they were going. He wished his parents would get him a car. They said he had plenty of time for a car and that he could get one when he could afford it—plus insurance. He hadn't figured out how he could get a job and still keep on the first honor roll at school. That had always be a priority with him from Kindergarten on through his senior year of high school.

"But you better be sure see that her dress and both feet are all the way in the car before you close the door."

Jack smiled at his dad and said, "Dad, I'm not stupid." He could tall by the look on his dad's face he shouldn't have said that. "Oops, sorry, Dad." His dad just grinned and shook his head and continued, "I remember closing your mother's dress in my dad's car door on our first date."

"Hey! You're kidding, right?"

His mom assured him, "No, he's not kidding. We were so glad I didn't get oil on it or that it didn't tear. Your dad was a real gentleman. He carefully opened the door and extracted my dress—unhurt."

"Just have to remember one thing, Jack," his dad said, "that she is your responsibility for the evening; you are to care for her and see that she is safe and is having a good time."

A whole new swarm of strange, warm feelings began to rise up inside of Jack.

His mom said, with a smile, "Your generation is very different from when we were dating but another thing that was important to me was that your dad—or my date, didn't leave me standing alone. I don't know how it is now but in our dating time it was so humiliating to be left standing all alone, not knowing where your escort was. It may be totally different now but it would have spoiled our whole evening; old fashioned, right?"

His mom said, "If the girls start whispering, Jack, you just should sort of step back and give her room. Then you can walk up to her when it looks like she is finished sharing with her friends. I'm sure that is still true today with you young people."

Jack had to grin as he said, "Girls are always doing that anyway." Jack could tell by the way his dad put his head down and smiled that his dad already knew that.

Jack's parents said he should ask Jill if she wanted to go get some refreshments or if she would like something to drink, as well, or whether she wanted to go with him or if Jack should go get drinks for both of them. Jack inwardly shook his head trying to sort all of that out, thinking, "boy, I ask one question and I get a whole book. Oh, well they mean well. I won't hurt their feelings."

Jack's dad reminded him to put a handkerchief in his breast or side pocket to give to Jill in case he should, at anytime, notice her starting to cry. From happiness--he thought, "Duh? How dumb is that?"

They reminded him to use his cell phone to keep in touch with Jill if they were separated. Jack was sure that would happen, because it seemed to him he often had to go find Jill when they were decorating the gym. Jack shared that with his parents, saying, "When I'd find her, she was usually helping someone." Jack was proud of Jill.

Unknown to Jack or Jill, both sets of their parents had previously gotten together and agreed on similar instructions for their son and daughter. They even had fun practicing as they reminisced about their senior prom. It took them back to their youthful years and the memorable time of their life when they were dating and falling in love. They all laughed together, realizing their children would most likely someday be surprised at learning of their collaboration.

Jill felt the next day was the hardest day of her life. It was hours before time to get dressed, but it seemed like torture to her to look at everything she would be wearing and not just put it on right away. The first thing of the day though, was a hair appointment at the beauty salon.

When Jill sat under the hair dryer one of the beauticians rolled a strange, low cart in front of her, took off Jill's shoes and socks, and put her feet in a little tub full of warm, soapy water. That felt good to her—strange, but good. Next the young lady took one of Jill's feet out of the water and dried it thoroughly.

Jill was then, a bit offended. She wasn't sure why she was getting her feet washed at a beauty shop.

Her mother had tried repeatedly to get her to come to this place, but Jill had begged off each time. She remembered hearing her father say, "Let her be a kid as long as possible." Jill had silently agreed.

Surprising Jill even more, the young lady in front of her on that little cart was using a file on her toenails. Jill leaned forward and looked two dryers down, where she saw another young lady busy doing the same thing for her mother. Catching her mother's attention she said leaned out from the hair dryer and smilingly said, "So this is why your feet always look so nice." She thought for few seconds and went on, "Maybe it isn't such a bad idea." The lady sitting between she and her mother took her head out from under the hair dryer and smiled radiantly.

She asked Jill, "How did your mother get you to come? I'd like to be able to talk my daughter into coming with me."

"Well, I couldn't hardly refuse; Mom says this is one of my graduation presents."

The lady started laughing, Jill's mom started laughing, Jill had to laugh, and soon all the rest of the ladies under their dryers tipped their dryers up to see what all the laughter was about. They couldn't really hear too much but by the looks on their faces the other ladies knew something was up.

Jill stopped laughing when the lady on the little seat asked her what color polish she wanted on her toes. That was too much; Jill started to say *none*. At that moment, a beautiful young lady walked into the shop in sandals; her toes were polished with white tips. Almost aloud she wondered, "How come I haven't paid attention to people's toes before?" she thought, "Maybe I am a bit of a heathen. Or maybe it's time for me to grow out of being a kid."

Next her mother took her to a ladies' clothing store, where they purchased several pair of panty hose.

"Mom, why are you getting those? I've never wanted to put those things on. I like my gym socks—oh, I guess they would look dumb with my dress and heels."

They then went to another department across the store, where a beautiful lady put a bunch of makeup on her face. She had noticed a lot of girls in her class wearing that stuff, and she had heard a couple of guys in their group make fun of them.

She pleaded with the lady, saying, "Don't put very much on; I don't want people to notice it on my face."

When she looked in the mirror, she didn't recognize the young girl looking at her. She liked all of it but the lip color. "Take it off," she pleaded. The lady applied a much lighter tone, and Jill was pleased.

Several days earlier, suspecting Jill would be going to the prom, Jill and her mother had gone shopping for shoes, and Jill got a new pair that she liked. The first time she tried to dance in her new heels with her dad, she stumbled. Trying to keep from falling, she grabbed hold of her father with a death grip, and they both went down on the floor in a heap.

"I might as well give up," she cried. "I will never be able to walk or dance in these dumb shoes."

"Jill," said her mother, "you have several days before the dance. I would suggest you just start walking in them around the house. It won't take long for you to get used to them."

Sure enough, Jill was soon walking, twirling, and prancing in her new heels.

Immediately after their supper, Jill started getting ready. Her mother asked her if she needed help. She shook her head no, then, said, "Come help me anyway, Mom."

Jill took one pair of the hose out of the package and just looked at them with disgust—dumb things, "why do girls wear those dumb things?" She stood while trying to pull one leg up, but she staggered, so she decided sitting would work better. Watching without being obvious, her mother remembered her own first pair of nylons.

Jill grabbed hold of the top and thrust one leg in. "Yikes, Mom, are they supposed to stretch like this?"

Her mother showed her how to gather the leg with her fingers, up to the toe end then slip them on her foot. Getting both legs on her feet, she gave a mighty pull, thrusting her fingernails through both sides of the top. She looked like she wanted to cry.

Jill's mother had half expected that. She quickly said, "No, no, Hon, don't worry; we have another pair."

Getting the other pair to her knees. Jill began to giggle, and so did her mom. Laughing brought more laughter, until they were laughing so hard the panty hose was in jeopardy.

Jill's cell phone rang. As she tried to stop laughing, she saw the call was from a girlfriend. "Hello, Stacy, are you ready? No? I'm trying to get a pair of panty hose on...what? I haven't either. No hose? Why didn't I think of that? We'll see you there. Bye."

First a startled look and then a smile crossed Jill's face. "Stacy isn't going to wear hose; neither is Penny or Lacy. If I don't wear those, my pretty toes will peek out of my open-toe shoes. Yeah!" Jill had to laugh inside, thinking about her toes being pretty.

Mother and daughter started laughing again. Soon they settled down and started making Jill look like a princess in her new dress.

Jack, of course, didn't know of the laborious, but fun, task of dressing that Jill and her mother experienced. As he dressed that evening he called his dad to see what he thought. Jack turned and looked in the mirror, not sure of what or who he was seeing.

Turning to his dad he said, "WOW! Dad, what's the saying about the clothes makes the man?"

His dad was proud of his son. It amazed him too; he was seeing a youth, turning into a man. Jack had really shot up the past year. He teased him a bit to loosen things up: "This may be a preview of what might take place in around ten years, son."

"What's taking place in ten years?"

"Well, most likely your wedding—you think."

"Wait a minute," said Jack, "let's not push that."

But Jack's dad could detect a faraway look in his son's eyes.

CHAPTER 6

High School Prom

A t Jill's house, her mom went to check on the camera, "Fred, you must come see your beautiful daughter. Come out, Jill, so your father can see how gorgeous you look."

Jill's father closed his eyes until she was standing in front of him in their living room. When he opened his eyes, they became clouded with tears. His little girl was no longer a kid; she was a young lady. "Where is my little girl?" he said. "Where has she gone?" Jill felt like she wanted to cry too. She felt bad, but she didn't feel bad enough to go back to jeans and tennis shoes for the prom.

She hugged her dear daddy and uttered, "Oh, Daddy, getting dressed up as I have just done is like magic to me. I can't remember ever having worn a dress like this one that mom made for me and Jack's special evening."

Jill's father hugged her back and assured her, "Honey, you go and have a lovely time this evening. It really wouldn't be a good idea for you to remain a child the rest of your life, but you will always be my little girl, even when you're married and have a husband and family." They both blew their noses and gave a few more sniffles. A knock at the door sent Jill flying into her bedroom to check her makeup and to have one more look in her full-length mirror.

Jack was thinking as he drove his dad's car to pick up Jill. He was all decked out in the tux and wondered how Jill would look. He was sure she would be the prettiest girl at the dance. After knocking on their door and stepping into the living room he saw an exquisite beauty come into the room. She took his breath away. He was speechless and just stood and stared like a dumb ox. His face felt numb and his arms hung like dead wood, he knew he acted like a clumsy oaf; he thought he might have even stuttered.

Likewise, there was a transformation in Jill's independent nature, which took a complete turnaround when she saw him dressed as a man. The two of them were suddenly aware of the same change in each other. They were both finally aware of Jack's height, for he was, at last, taller than her. How come she hadn't noticed that before? It was such a surprise that they just stood gaping at one another.

When Jack tried to pin his flower to Jill's dress, she kept laughing nervously and moving. Her mom finally had to do it, for Jack was shaking and was also laughing too much. As they went out the door Jack remembered his dad's words of instruction. At the top of the three steps, he held out his arm. Jill giggled a cute laugh and tucked her hand in the crook of his arm.

Standing inside at the door, Jill's parent's watched their little girl become a graceful young lady. They gave one another a special embrace. Their hearts swelled with pride and love for their adorable beauty that was gliding down the steps on the arm of a young gentleman they trusted with their daughter. They felt a satisfaction and trust in her escort.

When they arrived at the dance Jack remembered what his Dad had so carefully emphasized about the car. He was to *carefully* park the car, turn off the key, and put the key in his *pocket*. He was lucky to spot a parking place. As he pulled the front wheels into the spot, another car came speeding up, trying to beat him to it. Its brakes screeched as it stopped just inches away from their side. Jill could possibly have been hurt badly or killed had they been hit as fast as he was going. The rambunctious driver backed up and drove away. Jack thought for sure the driver had to have been drinking, as he and the others in the car were laughing and screaming like crazy.

Jill wiped her eyes with the back of her hand. "Jack, that was a miracle!" Jack had to agree. He thought of Shiny Man and almost expected to hear him speak, but Jack thought Jill's guardian angel was close at hand for her. (Matt 18:10 Take heed that ye despise not one of these little ones; for I say unto you, That in heaven their angels do always behold the face of my Father which is in heaven.)

Jack felt like a dunce afterward because he had forgotten to give Jill the handkerchief in his breast pocket. He had really missed out on impressing Jill there.

Jack pulled the rest of the way into the space and remembered again what his dad had said about the keys and about how his dad had closed his mom's dress in the car door on their first date. He offered his hand to Jill as she got out of the car. Jack had wondered if she would even take it, but he was elated when she did, she even took his arm as they walked to the door of the gym!

Talk about walking on a cloud. There couldn't have been anyone there that night happier or prouder than Jack—and probably Jill! As they danced together their steps blended as if they had often danced together. Jack would have loved to just stood to watch Jill twirl and sway, she looked so beautiful. His eyes and smile told Jill how proud he was of her. Jill was the one to suggest they go to the refreshment table. The P.T.A. had outdone themselves with refreshments. She even pointed to where the sodas were and didn't even do any whispering with her girl friends.

Many stayed to help clean up things after the dance was over, and of course the fun evening continued to the end, until everything was put back where it belonged. When Jack and Jill left the building, they were tired and ready to go home. As they and others got into their cars, they passed around noisy good-byes and waves.

The two soon arrived at Jill's home. Jack walked her up to the door and opened it for her. Jill called out, "We're back."

Jill's mom and dad came from the kitchen to hear all about how the prom had gone. Her dad went to the refrigerator and dished up a large bowl of ice cream for everyone while Jill changed into her jeans and T-shirt, took the pins out of her hair, letting it fall around her shoulders. Jack tried not to stare. He shed his coat, tie, and shoes. Eating their ice cream and sharing everything about their evening was almost as much fun as the prom itself. Jill loved the way her mom and dad laughed together.

That evening created a complete change in Jack and Jill's regard for one another. From that day forward, they saw each other in a different way. Jack said to himself, "Hey, man, is this what it feels like to fall in love?"

That summer was a far different summer than they had ever known before. It was like they had grown up overnight and become aware of one another in a new and exciting way. Jill learned the feminine way of not working at being better in everything than Jack. Jack felt tender and protective, though he was still in awe of Jill. As they prepared to go to college, they promised to wait for one another and to write every day.

CHAPTER 7

College and Heartfelt Declaration

The day arrived for Jack and Jill to go to their respective colleges. Jill was going to a Christian business College in Asheville, NC. Jack was going to another near N.C. for Journalism. Their flights were on the same day, though Jill was flying out an hour earlier, so they were taken to the airport together. Their parents rented a rather large van together, in order to get all six bodies in, plus all the stuff the two offspring had gathered to take with them.

Sitting, waiting for Jill's flight, she and Jack felt speechless. The realization hit them that they wouldn't be seeing one another the next day, or the day after that.

Jill decided she wanted a bottle of water to take on the plane so she asked Jack to go with her to get one. As they walked together to find a vendor, Jack stopped and put his hand on her arm. She turned to him, as he cautiously put his arm around her waist. Acutely realizing he was holding back the words he wanted to say and had been wanting to say to her for what seemed like, all of his life, he gently pulled Jill closer and blurted out, "Jill, I do … I do. Jill, I love you."

"Well, finally, you big dummy. I love you too, but I just wasn't going to be the one to say it first."

Jack pulled her close, picked her up around the waist, and whirled her around as she wrapped her arms around his neck and kissed him.

"This is absolutely unbelievable, Jill. I've never kissed you. I've always wanted to but was afraid you'd clobber me."

"Well, you don't have to worry; I promise not to. Although I might if you don't." He kissed her again and again then set her down on the floor. Jill asked Jack, "So, am I your girlfriend then?"

Jack thought for a moment, finally saying, "I'd like to say your more than my girlfriend? I'd like to say you're my fiancée—aren't you?

"Well, sure, remember in kindergarten you said you were going to marry me. I have never forgotten that and thought that was settled."

As Jack set Jill down on the floor they noticed a young couple walking towards them. The girl was pregnant and the guy had his arm around her shoulders as she smiled up at him.

The couple walked on, oblivious to Jack and Jill's notice of them. Jill looked up at Jack and whispered, "I hope they are married and have been married at least nine months."

Still looking up at Jack, she felt she knew he was thinking the same thing she was. Sometime before going to college, they had talked at length with counselors, and with one another, about each wanting to wait for sex until they were married; they had even exchanged promise rings. They were aware of some girls in high school who would get pregnant and go away for months at a time. Some came back with a baby, others came back without one. There was always a dark, sordid, mystery about it all, instead of something Holy and beautiful. One girl in particular caused them to open up and talk about the girl's situation. She had brought a baby back home with her. Her life had changed. She wasn't as care free and happy. She didn't go out with the same kids anymore. Each time, as word got around about such things, Jill became more determined than ever that she wanted to be a virgin when she got married.

With a serious look on his face, Jack took her hand, and they walked back to her boarding place. She looked up to him as they walked. "Thank you, Jack. You are the greatest guy I know, and I love you all the more."

Very seriously, Jack answered, "The same goes for me, Jill. I love you more than I can say. This makes me think of what my mom used tell me—that we are to give thanks to God for all things; that's in Ephesians five, verse twenty. I have to give Him thanks for our seeing that couple, back there. It has strengthened my pledge to you."

Today they would be parting for a time, and their good-byes, along with the parents were filled with heavy emotions. Jack was still unaccustomed to tears from Jill; he did have a handkerchief handy. Jill smiled as he gave it to her. She didn't give it back to him but stuck it in her purse. It had his initials on it. He gathered her in his arms for another quick embrace.

They didn't have much more time before parting--she had to get checked in. Turning to her mom and dad, the tears started to fall--for her as well as her mother; her dad worked at keeping them back. There were long embraces—Jack's parents walked up to her and exchanged fond hugs and well wishes. Turning back to Jack, they stressed again to one another, with eagerness, that they would be sure to write every day. It was time—she had to go---she would just make her boarding time. One last kiss and she was mixed in with all the other passengers rushing to make their flight. She was really gone from him. He wanted to run after her and talk her into waiting for the next flight. Jack pulled his eyes away from the spot Jill had disappeared into. He glanced at his dad who gave him a slight thumbs-up. He walked over and sat down by him.

Looking at his dad he found it hard, trying to keep tears from welling up in his eyes. His dad gave him a soft squeeze on his shoulder. That was the closest moment he had ever felt to his dad. He gave him a slow grin. His dad grinned back at him and gave him a man-to-man soft slap on the back. Jack smiled broadly, stood up and took a shaky breath. He was pulling himself together, making ready for the same kind of adventure as Jill. It was an anxious time in his life, parting from his parents into the mysterious event of adulthood. He, too, as they came to him with their arms around one another's waist, could see the both of them, struggling to release him to his right to go forth –to grow up.

Parting in the fall was painful for that young couple, as they had been together for the greater part of their lives, starting with a childhood love in kindergarten. Now they would be far apart in different colleges in different states.

Every minute of the first few days were filled with getting settled. That first evening, they wrote about all the head-spinning details of their day: getting settled in their dorm rooms, meeting their respective roommates, getting needed text books and supplies, learning where each classroom was located. They wrote especially about missing one another.

Jill's was filled with lamentations about missing Jack, but also stories about the excitement and newness of college life, and minute details of her dorm room and how many similar things, she and her roommate had brought.

Jack's were very similar, along with things Jill had mentioned in her letter. Jack poured out in another letter, the love he felt for her, "Jill, Angel, I should have told you long time ago how much I have always loved you. I was so lucky to fall in love with you in Kindergarten and have always loved only you. I especially have to warn you to be careful of all the wolves that will be looking for girls to date."

"Jack, Darling, I just can't tell you how exceedingly pleased I am to find that many of my classes are about things I had been doing at my father's office. Do you remember how many evenings, while I was still in high school, I went with my mom to my dad's office to help out? Now I find I will be studying most of the things that I touched on in daddy's office. Can you even imagine how happy I am, that college won't be as hard as I thought it would be. I just wish you were here. I love you and miss you so much." Jill was happy and sad at the same time.

Jack's return letter described how his classes would be introducing him to the ways of giving the newspaper's readers the political and social news of what was happening in the world. He had to learn how to deliver the news in an exciting way so people would want to follow his stories. This would boost sales and bring the newspaper more readers. It was all so exciting, and they both did well at keeping up with the required work. By the end of the year, both he and Jill were both pleased to share that college wasn't an impossible challenge for them.

The days hurried by and the last week of school, Jill was disappointed to learn that her parents had planned to spend the summer, clear across the country, at her uncle and aunt's home in Seal California, at Seal Beach. Why?"

Jill had to call her parents, "Mom, I got your letter. Why are you going to spend the summer at Aunt Anna and Uncle Jack's? Oh, I'm sorry—Hello, why are you going to do that?"" She could hardly wait for her mother to answer her, "I won't get to see Jack if you and Daddy do that--but I will, of course, come to be with you." Jill was already so yearning to see Jack, she didn't see how she was going to survive if she didn't get to be with him, come summer break. "Can't they come to see is at our home in S.C, instead?" She finally took a breath.

Jill—Honey--uh—JILL--are you listening, Honey?"

Oh, yes, I'm sorry, Mom." Panic was pushing at her heart, but she didn't want to be a jerk at this sudden news.

"I'm sorry, Mom. Can they come to South Carolina, instead?"

"Sweetheart, Your father has been suffering some long periods of fatigue, and Dr. Young has suggested he get away from his work for a rest. He really has been pushing himself for sometime. Getting completely away from his work to rest with his brother and Aunt Anna will be good for him. They have invited us to come be with them. They are *encouraging* us to come--a lakeside rest will be good for him. We hoped you would go with us. Jack will be welcome to come along. Honey, your father needs to get away."

Jill was stunned, "Oh, Mom, I'm so sorry. Why didn't you tell me sooner, I would have come right home."

"That's why we didn't tell you. We wanted you to finish the year. Daddy stayed home for a week. That didn't work, he just continued wanting to 'go in for just an hour or two' but that didn't work. He just kept worrying about what was going on at the office. You will come be with us then?"

There was no hesitation. She knew she had to go—she wanted to go—with them. A letter was sent to Jack telling him of the events, inviting him to join them for all of the trip or part of it.

Having a determination before he even went to college, to help with the expense of his education made the invitation impossible. Jack did not want to put the heavy expense of college on his parents. He had, before leaving for college, secured a place to work in his hometown, in S.C. for five days a week during summer break through to the last week before returning to school.

Jack answered the invitation with a letter of thank you and a decline, explaining why--then a phone call. He just had to hear Jill's voice, to tell her he loved her. He was so disappointed he wouldn't get to be with her and hold her. He had to further explain to her about getting the summer job and why--to help pay for his education even though his parents planned for it.

"Jack, I'm so glad you called. I've missed you so much and looked forward to being together, but don't feel badly, Darling. If my daddy's parents hadn't set money aside for my education, I most likely would have planned the same thing."

" Thank you, Angel, for understanding. I will call you on the weekends and that will help take some of the loneliness away."

"That will be wonderful, and let's put a time limit on how long we will talk; that will also save money."

Jack's heart swelled with love as he realized and appreciated her sweet thoughtfulness. That gave him the grateful impression she was not a spendthrift. He sure didn't want to start their married life in debt.

He was disappointed that Jill wouldn't be home for summer but understood her feelings about wanting to be with her parents, especially since her father was having health problems. He told Jill, "I will come some weekends to visit with you and your family."

He did go for several short weekends and was able to meet her aunt and uncle. There were also often, other family members at the lake as well, so Jack got to meet more of Jill's family. His parents were invited to come as well and were asked to stay longer than Jack was able to stay.

Jack wasn't going to be able to do that very often for Air travel was expensive, taking much of the money he had hoped to apply to his college tuition so didn't go many times.

In the fall Jill's parents went back to S.C. and Jill was encouraged by her parents to return to college. The second year at school rolled along pretty much the same as the first year. Jack and Jill continued to do well with their classes and kept in touch daily with letters. The phone calls and a couple weekends together at Seal Beach had greatly helped them keep up their spirits.

Jill's father was still suffering from deep fatigue, so he and his wife were at the lake with Jill's uncle for the second summer and part of the winter. However, he began to feel stronger, so they moved back home to take care of his Investment Business during the Christmas holidays.

CHAPTER   8

Lack of Communication - Graduation

When Christmas break rolled around Jack and Jill were back home. Jill was able to help her father at his office, but she and Jack still got to be together, having fun with their old friends before hurrying back to school when it was time, for the rest of the semester.

At the beginning of Jack's junior year, a newspaper became interested in this young man whom many of his teachers were impressed with. He was offered a very impressive job upon graduation, but in order to take it, he would have to fit two more special subjects into his already *full schedule*. He planned to keep the job and fantastic salary as a surprise for Jill, until they graduated. Jack's grades had been good through grade school, high school and the first two years of college, and he intended for it to continue that way--even with the extra needed classes--through to his college graduation.

Returning to their respective colleges, Jack and Jill began writing letters again, each day.

As assignments for all of his regular classes, plus the two extra classes, began to heap upon Jack, time was taken away from writing letters plus his sleep and eating. The need for extra hours of study and work took from him any time for relaxation. There soon seemed to be no time for anything but classes, study, and turning in assignments. His letters to Jill began to grow further apart. Jill, still writing daily, mildly complained to him, urging him to write more often. She was disappointed at first with his response, but she forgave him when the longed-for letters came. It became the pattern, and Jill tried to reconcile herself to it. She found herself wondering, "What does Jack do when he isn't in class or studying?"

Letters from Jack became even further apart, and Jill was again and again disappointed. She wasn't going to try making him write if he didn't want to. There was no way for her to understand Jack's workload, but being pretty self-determined, she buried herself in her studies.

By their mid-junior year, the letters that Jack wrote were shorter and less personal than they had been. He wasn't getting enough sleep, barely had time to go for meals, and was having a hard time knowing what to write to Jill; he didn't know what to say to her. Jack didn't love her any less, but he was struggling to keep up with all of his assignments and his reading material and didn't want to burden her with his problems. He reasoned to himself that Jill was most likely in the same boat, considering all the work she, too would have to keep up with.

Come summer they again didn't get to see one another—things seemed to be working against them. Jill's father was no longer able to work. They knew they had to be patient. Jill's aunt and uncle wanted Jill's parents to come stay with them permanently. They talked Jill's mom and dad into coming to live in California.

Jill's dad was forced to turn his business over to his lawyer, to hire someone dependable to manage the office temporarily. Jill and her mom flew back and forth occasionally to take care of things at the office--things that needed the owner's attention. Since her mom had worked as needed for many years in the office, as had Jill, she was capable of overseeing business matters. Jill then, found herself commuting, along with her mother, back for a few days at a time, working at her father's office.

Commuting back and forth was beginning to be hard for Jill's mom, so they decided to move back to their home for the summer. Jill was then possibly busier than Jack at his summer job, for she and her mother took turns being at the office or at home so that one of them would be home with Jill's father during the daytime hours. He wasn't doing well.

Wanting to help out somehow, Jack started bringing lunch to Jill, her dad and himself, when it was her day to be home. He started doing it more often because her father enjoyed visiting with Jack. Jill was again convinced Jack did love her. Her dad's health was not good at all so they both equally agreed to limit their evening dates, for Jill worried about him when she and Jack went out.

Jack's mom and dad often came with Jack when he would visit Jill's family for the evening. They were a little hesitant at first, about coming, but Jill's mom encouraged them to come often, for Jill's father loved to have them and was even more peaceful and relaxed when they came; he enjoyed the man company—the man conversation.

Jack did take the last two weeks off of his summer job before the start of his senior year began. He accepted the suggestion of his parents to spend that time with them at Myrtle Beach ocean side vacation spot in S.C., where Jack's uncle and aunt lived. They invited Jill to go with them but of course, weren't surprised when she felt she had to decline.

Jack and Jill then had a renewal of sorts, with letters—they started the daily—or almost daily—letters again. Jack being able to write two letters to Jill's one, much better at that time than Jill was able to do. There were phone calls, but they were still many miles apart. They wrote of their love for one another, making plans for all the wonderful things they would do when they could be together again for good and discussing how wonderful their lives would be when they were finished with college. Jack finally told her about the two extra courses he had crowded in with his other courses, saying they were important courses he would need, but he still managed to keep from Jill, as a surprise, the job offer with the incredible starting salary he would have when he graduated.

As the fall term was approaching, Jill told her parents she was not going back to college. She would not think of leaving her with her father so ill. This news upset her dad terribly. So much so, it looked like he was in danger of a heart attack. What was she to do?

"Daddy you are more important to me than any college education. I want to stay home with you and Mom. With total rest you will get better, then I can go back to finish."

The more she talked the more upset he became until she finally agreed to go back and finish. With great trepidation she packed and left—her whole being, torn within herself. It was almost impossible to study much less, attend classes.

Within a week Jill's mother wrote encouraging letters to Jill about her father. The doctor had insisted that her father must make up his mind to retire permanently from his job and hire someone to take over the office so Jill's mom could stay home with him. The doctor felt that if he would do that, he could enjoy a good number of more years and possibly be able to go see his daughter graduate from college. It tore her father up to think of give up working at the business he loved, but the thought of seeing Jill graduate encouraged him to comply. He had in the back of his mind, a teasing thought that Jack might be able to take over his business when he graduated from college—he never mentioned that thought, to anyone—yet. His health improved at that possibility; he gave in and began to enjoy retirement.

Jill's news from her mother made a heavy load drop from her heart. She thanked God, for she felt everything was going to be all right. She could again tackle her studies with confidence and pleasure. Things were fine at first. Jack wrote cheerful and loving letters fairly regular. They helped to make her feel secure and happy.

But for Jack it was the same struggle. He wished he had registered to take those two extra needed classes during the summer. This caused more pressure for him. His mind twisting with the decisions he tried to reason within himself. He was sensible though, telling himself, "If I did that I would not have been able to work at my summer job and have money to put towards my tuition, plus I would have to explain to Jill the possibility of having to tell of my surprise."

"Jill, please help me to know for sure what to do, okay?" Jack's parents were only a few years from retirement with a comfortable retirement to take care of them, for the rest of their lives. Explaining his situation to her eased his mind a bit.

He was relieved at Jill's wisdom, "Jack, we are young and have many years ahead of us. You have made the right decision," she told him, "your dad may think he should keep working, in order to pay your tuition if you had not worked to help a great deal with payments. Yes, they have money set aside to take care of your college tuition, but that will be a nice part of their retirement, making it more comfortable for them to enjoy things that otherwise they may not have been able to do. "I'm proud of you, Darling, you have good heart."

Jack too returned to college with a lighter heart, even more determined to carry out his plan. He still did not have to reveal his surprise to Jill. Starting his senior year he looked forward to it. He was ready for the work that waited for him upon graduation-- a comfortable life, free of money problems.

When Jack went back to school, he was surprised for he was alone in his room. The fellow who was to have been his roommate had dropped out of college at the last minute. At first he liked being alone, but it really wasn't good, because Jack became isolated and had no one to talk to. He and Jill wrote faithfully, but as Jack struggled to keep up with his assignments, his letters to her again became further and further apart. Jill again was disappointed about the lack of letters she received from him. She just did not understand him when they were apart.

When they wrote all the letters during the summer, Jack had explained somewhat about his heavy load of classes, but he hadn't told Jill just *how* hard it had been the past year or that it would be just as heavy during his senior year. As his letters began to be shorter, further apart and not as loving; her letters began to change also. He was sure she too, was working hard to keep up with her classes, so he didn't think much about the change in her letters.

He was grateful for the encouraging letters he got from home, which helped keep him going. He was struggling to keep a positive attitude toward the goal he was working so hard for. As graduation time came closer, he had hopes of seeing the light at the end of the tunnel. He would be able to eat and sleep again like he should, get some rest, and regain the weight he had lost. He would be able to be with Jill again. He hoped he hadn't made a mistake by not confiding in her about his workload *and* news of the promised job. He so wanted the job to be a great surprise.

But around the middle of the year loneliness started to affect Jill's health, and grades. Depression began to play a foul work on Jill. She and her roommate, Linda, had developed a close friendship, and Linda was concerned for Jill but didn't want to pry. She found herself gazing aimlessly out their window, thinking about Jill. She could tell something was wrong but didn't know what to do—or whether to do anything. She felt that perhaps it would be best to stick to her studies and not try to heal the world.

When she discovered Jill was skipping classes and sleeping more and more, she knew, in the name of friendship, that she had to do something. A person didn't see someone drowning and just turn the other way. One weekend she casually suggested they share a pizza, saying she didn't want to go alone. Jill rather reluctantly dragged herself out of bed and agreed to go. Linda noticed she had slept in her clothes and was going to go without even giving her hair attention with a comb.

Something was very, very wrong. They ate and talked, and Linda found several opportunities to ask innocent questions. Without warning, Jill covered her face in her hands. Her shoulders began to shake as she started to sob uncontrollably. As a close friend and roommate, Linda was not too surprised at Jill breaking down, though it was unlike Jill to do so. Linda moved to the seat in the booth next to her friend. Slowly and tenderly, she eased her arm around Jill's shoulder and waited. Word by word, Jill exposed her hurt feelings. Jack had dumped her.

Being a psychology major, Linda knew not to push. She had seen from the beginning how much Jill cared for Jack. She patiently waited for Jill to share as much as she wished. Her observations told her of some issues that could become rather detrimental to Jill's future. When Jill had mildly complained again to Jack about his letters, he had stopped writing. Jill felt dumped. Linda wondered if she could help Jill in some way.

After they finished their pizza, Jill became more relaxed and glad of her friendship with Linda. Giving Linda a light hug she told her, "Linda, I am so grateful to you for the friend you have been. What would I have done without you caring for me." She silently thanked God for putting the two of them together.

When they stood to go pay for the pizza and get back to school, a friend of Linda's was leaving also. Linda introduced the two girls. "Emma, this is my roommate and good friend, Jill." Emma offered a hug and Jill immediately felt better.

As the three of them left the pizza place and were walking

together, Emma told Linda about a beach party they were getting up that evening and asked Linda to come.

"Are you free?" she asked Linda. "Could you come?" She indicated that Jill was invited too.

"How about it, Jill? Want to go together?" Wow, thought Linda, "this is really timely."

It didn't take much encouragement to get Jill to accept. A smile crept across her face, and she nodded yes. "I'd love to. Thank you for asking." Jill almost danced her way back to school.

The beach party was fun and Jill immediately felt accepted by those in the group. She soon realized they were a Christian group.

School became enjoyable for Jill again, and her grades immediately improved. She was even able to make up some work. Along with the burden of loneliness off her shoulders, her health also improved. She wasn't nearly as tired, for she was sleeping better at night and eating better. She was offered more invitations to do things with the group and began meeting many other students. She felt alive again.

One fellow, named Phil, began singling her out, making her feel wanted and attractive. With each get-together, he became more attracted to her. He wanted just the two of them to date, though he had seen Jill's promise ring. Phil never tried rushing her, but he made it evident that he was caring for her more and more.

Jack's final grades were all in but one, and were excellent. He had already, been told by his prof though, that he had aced that class also. He could finally find time to breathe. He sent a letter to Jill telling her he hoped her finals hadn't been too hard and that he hoped she was happy with her grades. He wrote that he knew it would be tricky trying to work it out time wise but suggested they try to attend one another's graduation exercises.

Jill though, felt it only fair to tell him she was interested in someone else and declined his offer.

Panic and heartbreak hit Jack hard—he felt dazed. Hurriedly he drew money from his savings account for a two-way flight ticket for the next weekend and rushed to find Jill. After having a heck of a time meeting up with her, he found her with another guy. He took her aside some distance from him and with absolute confidence in her forgiving him, told her of all the plans he had been working at to qualify for a fantastic job. With that job, he could buy her a beautiful house so she wouldn't have to work and a new car for each of them. She could have the beautiful wedding that she dreamed of and had only to plan for it. They would have the future they had dreamed of some years ago.

When Jill found out Jack's seemingly heartless plans, and when she noticed he said nothing about how he actually felt for her, she was so startled she could hardly talk to him.

As he tried to explain everything to her, her face seemed to come alive with understanding. "So my future with you would be living in a beautiful house with a work-alcoholic husband. No thank you. You just go be married to your job. I want no part of it."

Jack was unbelieving as Jill took the arm of her crummy new boyfriend, turned, and hurried away, becoming lost in the crowd of students around them. There was nothing for Jack to do but hurry to the airport and return for his graduation ceremony. He just barely caught his flight. Back at school, he was absolutely stunned to find he had been living a dream alone. He had to run to get in line. He grasped the fact that instead of trying to surprise Jill, he should have shared something to keep her sure of him.

Jack passed the rest of the moments before his graduation in a daze. Receiving his diploma held no satisfaction for him.

Thinking of what was waiting for him gave Jack another thrust of energy and drive; he would get established in the routine of the new job and pray that Jill would forgive him and give him another chance. He was not at all impressed with the guy Jill had been dating. He could plainly see through that fellow--he was not good enough for her.

CHAPTER 9

New Expectations

Jill's graduation was coming up, and graduate's were starting to make plans for the future. Phil was ever so attentive, always wanting to get away from the others. He wanted Jill to himself. He made plans for a romantic dinner with dancing afterward. Jill was sure he would propose that evening.

Exams were over, and Jill was pleased with her grades. Jill and Phil sat together holding hands, at the graduation ceremony, both looking forward to their evening together.

When Phil picked her up, he looked so handsome, and she could see in his eyes he loved her and was proud of how beautiful she looked in a special gown chosen just for him. Dinner was perfect and all they had hoped for; the music the band played was extra dreamy. Phil suggested a walk to enjoy the lovely grounds the restaurant was situated on. There was a gorgeous lake and a walk all around it. He took her hand, and their fingers entwined. He led her off the path to a small grassy knoll, sat down, and put his handkerchief on the ground so she could sit without getting any grass stains on her elegant dress. Jill was impressed at how thoughtful he was. "Such a polished gentleman, she thought, and what a beautiful place this is."

His arm around her shoulders gave her a feeling of peace and safety. She almost held her breath, knowing he was going to propose.

Phil then surprised her by wanting to lie back, and by his unexpected and insistent exploration of her shoulder straps. Her remark, "Phil, don't do that!" brought more tugging at her back zipper. As she tried to sit up, he eased her back down. He began kissing her in a different way than he ever had before, and he pressed into her as he pulled all the more at her dress, giving her a strange feeling about what was going on. As she pushed him away, he became even more forceful, tearing at her dress. A sudden realization dawned on her. He had set her up. His aim was to score that evening.

Seeing another couple passing by she screamed loudly, "Help" calling to them.

Phil tried to put his hand over her mouth, but she jerked it away. "Help me, please, help m …help!" Phil jumped up and disappeared into the shadows, leaving his handkerchief behind.

The young man ran up to answer Jill's call for help. He understood immediately what was happening when he saw Phil running away. Helping her down from the knoll to the walkway and over to a young lady, he introduced her as his wife. Being a tender, compassionate, person, she put her arms around Jill to comfort her. Jill was shaking so badly she was having a hard time standing. She became almost hysterical with the realization of what could have happened to her. She might have even been found drowned in the lake the next morning.

Gratefulness tumbled from Jill's lips. "Oh, I'm so glad you were here. Thank you," she gasped, "thank you so much. Thank You, Lord God!" Her legs kept threatening to buckle under her, and she couldn't stop shaking. The lady held Jill as she fought to gain control of herself.

"Here, dear, let me help put your clothes back together."

The pain Jill felt about what might have happened hit her hard. Drying her tears, she gave way to anger at Phil. "That creep, he *never* tried anything like that before."

Her body started shaking again. Talking calmly to Jill the young man and his wife urged her to return to the dance with them. She agreed to it, and as they helped her calm down, she began to enjoy the rest of the evening. She silently wondered what Jack was doing.

The couple got to know Jill as the evening wore on, and were impressed with her fine mannerisms. They were intrigued to learn that she had just that day graduated from college. In order to carry on a pleasant conversation, the man explained they were there on business. When Jill excused herself and went to the ladies' room, his wife suggested he find out more about her and her studies.

As they chatted upon Jill's return, they learned of the classes she had taken and, with clever inquiry by the wife, about her grades.

Here, in this young lady seemed to be an answer to Mr. James Tyler's need. With an interested look and subtle nod of her head, the wife smiled lovingly at her husband. He understood his wife's secret suggestion and offered Jill a trial job as his secretary, with the possibility of a promotion to other higher responsibilities. "My present secretary is taking permanent leave," he said, "for she and her husband are expecting their first baby, and she wants to be home to care for their child. My generous wife has been filling in for me."

The evening ended pleasantly, and they were so grateful that Jill was safe, but they wished Phil could have been arrested. They delivered Jill safely back to her dorm. Upon inquiring at the men's dorm they learned that Phil had left town. Not wanting to possibly draw unpleasant attention to Jill, they dropped their inquiry

CHAPTER 10

New Life New Job

Jack passed the rest of the moments before his graduation in a daze. Receiving his diploma held no satisfaction for him.

He was glad he didn't have to report for his new job immediately. Luckily the job was in his hometown in S.C. He was so worn out and needed time to get caught up, with needed sleep and rest. Thinking of what was waiting for him gave Jack a new hope, another thrust of energy and drive. He would get established in the routine of the new job and pray that Jill would forgive him and give him another chance. He was not at all impressed with the guy Jill had been dating. He could plainly see that that fellow was not near good enough for her. The idea came to him to keep an eye out in other newspapers to see if Jill would announce an engagement to that no good guy.

Upon starting his new job, Jack poured all of his heart and energy into it. A couple of months into the job, however, he began to see that it was really a sad disappointment. He found it a strenuous job that lasted all day long and often late into the evening. Jack was constantly in and out of his car, never settling anywhere more than a few minutes. The weekends continued the stress with big breaking stories. Much of Jack's time was spent traveling—mostly out of the country. His eating and sleeping habits was slowly killing him. He guessed he wasn't cut out for newspaper reporting. His struggle to get a good night's sleep was worse than it had been when he was in college. He discovered, this was because of a shortage of staff. There was nothing he could do except work harder. He began having digestive problems. He knew he wasn't able to sit quietly and eat balanced meals. It was always on the run, picking up here and there what he could find, many times in questionable eating-places.

It didn't take too much longer for Jack to know it was not the job for him, especially when he wanted to start over with Jill—if she would accept him back and hopefully forgive him and marry him. What kind of life would it be like with a new wife if he were working long hours, being called up often in the middle of the night—even out of the country--because of some great breaking story, and having to report at the office the minute he got back? Was the great salary worth it? Would it be fair to Jill?

Oftentimes, when he would get to the scene of something happening, some of the people there would be angry that reporters had shown up. At other times a number of people at the scene might want to get into the news and would make it impossible to figure out what was really happening. He had been knocked down in erratic crowds, his cameraman's camera had been broken, and he had been shot at and spit on. What was he going to do? Jack's life had surprisingly, suddenly turned very difficult, to say the least. He felt so alone.

After more of the same workweek, it was a Sunday, and Jack needed to get away. He took a drive out into the country to escape. He couldn't make sense out of what was supposed to be the perfect job. His mind was such a jumble that he didn't feel safe driving on the highway. He wished for the company of Shiny Man right then.

Finding an inviting grassy spot along the highway, just beyond an overpass, he pulled over and got out. He walked back to the overpass and leaned onto the warm, concrete rail, pondering all his problems. Looking out, there seemed to be a young forest of trees at first glance, but as Jack looked straight down, he could see nothing but a dirty, barren, dry creek bed below. He felt he was looking down at his life—a place of hopelessness with nothing but waste and a lot of stuff that had been neglected and thrown away. Jack took Jill's little picture out of his shirt pocket and felt tears coming. It was an after thought that morning when he put the picture in his pocket. As he wiped his eyes with the back of his hand, her picture slipped from his grasp and fell below.

Feeling a gripping panic, he raced down the embankment to retrieve the picture. There before his eyes were people, scattered in the shade of the trees, all as desperate-looking as the debris. Jack seemed to be as much of a surprise to them as they were to him. He felt his life was absolutely falling apart.

This was Jack's first time to happen upon a group of homeless people, and it was purely by accident. Jack stared at them, and they in turn stared back at him. No one moved as he slowly stooped and picked up Jill's picture. He held it up and waved it. Had they seen it fall to the ground? A couple of them smiled a weak smile out of the sides of their mouths as Jack turned and retreated up the embankment. He looked down again and saw that none of them seemed to have moved. He wondered why he hadn't seen them before he went down there.

Jack climbed into his car, swung it around and headed back to town. An image burned itself into his memory. It was the image of a big man—the biggest man he had ever seen. He seemed to be somewhat apart from the other homeless people, almost *under* the overpass. There had been a foul smell as Jack walked over and picked up Jill's picture; he wondered if the odor came from that fellow. How glad he was that the big guy hadn't come after him. He looked almost like a bear—a big, shaggy, fierce bear.

As he drove back to town, Jack felt no better. He still felt like walking. He parked his car again and got out to walk off some of the tension and confusion of the news-coverage violence, his hatred of his work, his missing Jill, and his experience with those gaunt-looking homeless people with the huge man.

Not having prayed for quite some time he reached out to God, "Help me Lord, please help me. Nothing seems to go right anymore. Help those homeless people back by the underpass, Lord, are they safe there?"

His imagination started working. Were those people being held there? But no, that couldn't be. It didn't make sense. He was intrigued by what he had seen there, but he wasn't sure why. Jack looked across the street he was walking on and noticed a bench at the curb—Shiny Man was sitting on the bench. He crossed the street to go to him and when he got there Shiny Man and the bench were gone. He thought, "Am I losing my mind?" He walked on, walking with no destination in mind, just thinking.

As he walked for quite some time, he became aware of music. There was singing, but it stopped after a moment and people began to pour out of a building and onto the sidewalk. With people all around him, he discovered he was in front of a church and was being engulfed with friendliness. Most of them didn't realize he was not a part of the congregation, but Jack couldn't help but respond to their smiles and handshakes. Some wished him a nice day, a couple told him where they were meeting for lunch and wanted to know if he needed a ride. He said, "Ah, no, … I've got my car, thanks."

As the crowd began to thin out, a message came to him—he had seen the words on a piece of paper just recently: "A kind word will keep someone warm for years." He was sure he would remember that incident. After all the people had left, he found a warm feeling inside. He was alone, wondering why he felt so good and so uplifted, and why he felt like laughing. He looked around, expecting to see Shiny

Man. The thought hit him that it was a good thing he had ended up in front of a church instead of a nightclub. Well, that didn't matter, because he wasn't a drinking man.

Looking around dismayed, Jack found that his car was nowhere in sight. Almost talking out loud, he wondered, "Where in the world is my car?" As he walked back and forth on the sidewalk, his memory slowly began to come back, and his mind began to fill in the blank spaces. When he finally realized just how far he had walked, he was almost stupefied for he was close to the downtown area. "How in the world did I walk this far?" He wondered how he had managed to get to that place in his stupor? Something had to change in his life.

A man came out of the church, walked to a sign in the yard and began to change some of the letters. In a moment, another man came out of the door and walked toward the man working on the sign. He saw Jack standing there on the sidewalk and went to greet him, to shake his hand with a smile. In spite of not knowing where he had left his car, Jack was feeling good, and the man's handshake made him feel like he wanted to know him better. Because of the man's collar, Jack assumed he was the pastor.

"Hello, I'm Pastor Ed. I don't believe I know you. Are you new here at church?"

"No, as a matter of fact I was just passing by when a lot of people started coming out of the church. They were such a happy group of people; they just started talking and shaking my hand. They didn't know I wasn't a member. I loved it."

"Hey, I'm glad to hear that." Pastor Ed was happy about his congregation's congeniality. He, too, was equally known for his friendly manner, and for being easy to talk to. He and Jack shook hands and exchanged a few words.

As Jack turned to go find his car, the pastor, with a catching smile in his voice, called to him: "Come back next Sunday and try us out." The pastor felt there was something different about this young fellow, something outstanding somehow. It was strange to have a feeling like that about someone he had just met and had exchanged so few words.

With a warm smile, Jack called back to him, saying, "I just might do that." Then, as a second thought, Jack took heart, turned, and said to him, "Have you had lunch yet?

What a coincidence, or perhaps a God-incidence, that was the same thought to hit Pastor Ed too. As the young man stood waiting, he answered "No I haven't! Do you have any good suggestions?" He offered up a quick prayer, quietly whispering, "Thank You, Lord!"

"Well, you know, I'm pretty good at coming up with ideas sometimes," said Jack. "Want to take a chance? I'm buying."

Since the pastor didn't have a lot of time right then, he suggested his regular eating place, which was a couple of blocks down the street. It was only a few minutes away, they wouldn't have to drive, and the food there was good.

As he walked towards the young man, Pastor quickly called his favorite prayer partner, his wife, to tell her what had just happened. "Would you like to bring our son and come join us?" She declined and urged her husband to go ahead and see if there was something he could do for the stranger.

Pleasant conversation accompanied an excellent sandwich and a cup of freshly brewed coffee. Jack felt at ease talking to this man. As they finished eating and went to pay the bill at the cash register, both Jack and the pastor knew that something out of the ordinary had taken place between them in that hour.

Outside the door, Pastor Ed stuck out his hand to Jack. "Thanks for lunch. Let's do this again real soon. I really mean that, Jack."

Slowly nodding his head and looking into the pastor's eyes, Jack felt the wisdom again in this understanding man, and he said in earnest, "I promise you I'll be seeing you again before too long." As they turned to go their separate ways, the pastor again whispered softly, "Thank You, Holy Spirit." He was confident about there being a spiritual companionship. He thought to himself, "What is there about this young man?"

However, as Jack walked away, he was strangely overcome with a gripping, overpowering sense of loneliness and depression. Without warning, his world seemed to freeze. He hated to think of going to work the following day. He had to get out of that job. He determined that he would resign in the morning, and no way was he going to see that pastor again either. Jack felt there wasn't anyone that could possibly begin to understand his situation. Jack had confided too much to that pastor about his dilemma—his helpless feeling of being deep in a dark hole that was pulling him in because of his all consuming love for Jill. His heartbreak and depression were caused by his not being able to locate her.

In the back of his mind he remembered hearing, "When we have found joy, the thief comes only to steal and kill and destroy. (John 10:10). He was sure he had heard that in church. No matter how depressed he was, he still had to find his car.

The temperature was climbing, and the farther he walked, the more he felt the sun on his back. He couldn't believe he had walked and not been aware of where he had parked. Hours later, he was still walking but hadn't found his car. Who could he call to help him?

CHAPTER 11

Law Enforcement on the Job

J ack finally called attention to himself, and a neighborhood watch member called the police to report a "suspicious-looking man" who appeared to be planning trouble, for he had passed her house three times.

Officer Stolke happened to be in the same vicinity and had also noticed him. He couldn't determine if the guy was lost, drunk, or for sure up to no good. He followed Jack from a good distance for about five more minutes before calling the station to inquire if there was another police car in the area. There was, and the other car was directed to come quietly from another direction.

Jack felt a loathing for himself for forgetting where he had parked his car, and he was getting madder by the minute, so when the two police cars pulled up beside him, he was in no mood for their intrusive presence.

As the other officer was sitting, observing Jack, Officer Stolke, stepped out of his car and walked toward the front of his car, keeping the car between himself and Jack. "Sir, you have been noticed walking back and forth in this neighborhood. Is there something we can help you with? What's your name?"

Jack was tired, hot, and hungry. He wanted to tell the officer to lock him up for a while, at least until he got himself together. "I'm a newspaper reporter. My name is Jack Hampstan," he shouted loudly in exasperation. "I've lost my car. I've been walking for hours trying to find it."

Nodding at the officer on the other side of the street, Officer Stolke directed Jack to get into his car and said they would see if they could find his car.

Feeling a bit kindly toward this fellow, Officer Stolke asked, "You seem to have a lot on your mind; what's going on with you?"

Jack put his arms on the dash, laid his head on his arms, and said, "Boy, wouldn't this make the front page. I feel like I could go out there like a frustrated little kid, lie down on that sidewalk, and throw a tantrum."

The policeman from the other car had climbed into the backseat of Officer Stolke's car. No one said anything for a few minutes. When Jack turned his face towards Officer Stolke, the one in the backseat touched him on the shoulder. As Jack turned toward him, he drew back and said, "Hey, I recognize you. Down at the poolroom, you were the reporter that got knocked down and almost got trampled, along with your cameraman and his camera. How on earth could you lose your car?"

The officers were sympathetic in listening to Jack's car problem. They had the station check to see if his car had been pulled in for some reason. The answer was negative. After both policemen in their own cars drove, looking for his car, they agreed it had most likely been stolen.

"Now we'll take you to a deserted area and you can get out and have your tantrum."

"No, I think I'll just sit here and bawl. That might be safer."

Jack had to grin in spite of himself. Officer Stolke took Jack to the police station to fill out a stolen car report.

The policeman taking all the particulars about his car dryly said to Jack, "I'm sorry to tell you this, but if it is found, it will probably be stripped and you'll have only a body. Some of the body parts may even be taken off."

Jack, who was slumped on a chair beside the officer filing his report, straightened up and thought a moment. "Thanks," he said. "That is just what I needed to hear. I feel so much better."

With a sideway grin, the officer stood up and put a hand on Jack's shoulder. "Yeah, I was sure that would make your day. We'll see what we can do for you, fella."

Officer Stolke offered to take Jack for a hamburger before taking him home, and Jack was all for that. McDonald's was a couple blocks away. As they pulled into the lot, Jack excitedly yelled and pointed. "Hey. There's my car!"

To Jack's surprise the officer drove right on through and out of the lot. He called, reporting they had found the car. A special unit was called in to apprehend the car thief and the car. They parked around the corner, out of sight from McDonald's.

"Hold on; be patient, Jack, that hijacker will be wanting to cruise his neighborhood, showing off his 'new car,' and we will be ready. "We'll wait him out. Here comes my backup."

"What happens now?" asked Jack

"Well," explained Officer Stolke, "you most likely already know some, if not all, of this: When the stolen vehicle is located, the handling officers will request back up and set up a containment around McDonalds, here, since that's where the car is, so the bad guys can't get away. They will also coordinate the containment so the bad guys inside could not see the police cars outside. The handling officers will put themselves in a position of advantage to watch the bad guys and remain undetected. The coordination will all take place over the police radio.

When those bad guys come out, the officers will let them get into the car. Once the bad guys are in the stolen car, the handling officers and back up units will come into the parking lot and position themselves behind the stolen vehicle. The positioning is called a felony car stop configuration. This is done to safely extract the bad guys from the stolen vehicle. The bad guys will be called back to the officers one at a time until the stolen car is empty. Each occupant will be handcuffed and placed into the backseat of a police car before the next bad guy is called out. Once the officers are confident that the stolen car is empty of additional people, they will approach it tactically to ensure it is in fact empty and secure the crime scene.

"WOW," said Jack, "I'm really impressed. I'm sure that takes months of training—makes me feel proud of you guys." Officer grinned and replied, "you're right and it takes a special kind of person to do the job.

Officer Stolke took Jack to the police station, where the suspects' pictures and fingerprints were being taken. Papers in the car proved ownership. Jack had to wait until all procedures were accomplished before getting his car back. He found it was unhurt, except for some very important wires that had to be put back in their rightful places. The carjacker and his friends were hauled off to a place where they would be sure not to steal another car—at least not for a long time.

While driving home, Jack worried about having no place to park but at the curb in front of his apartment. He had to trust it would be there in the morning. All he could do was make sure it was locked when he got out of it. Bed was going to feel mighty good, for his body was almost spent. He slept soundly for ten hours and woke wondering about his job at the newspaper office. He still hated to think of going in, but he did give thanks that he had gotten his car back undamaged.

Getting to work late the next morning and casually mentioned seeing the homeless group by the underpass, the editor jumped on it. Jack was to go get pictures and interview each one of them to find out about their lives—that would make a good human-interest story.

"In other words, invade their privacy and plaster their lives all over the paper for the world to gawk at?" said Jack. "No thanks." That went against the grain with him. When the boss insisted that he was to do that, Jack turned in his resignation, and no amount of persuasion could change his mind, not even a raise in salary. He gathered his things and walked out to put them in his car--his car was gone again.

Jack's car was never found, not even a trace of it. Perhaps that would have been the time to lie down on the sidewalk and have the tantrum. Jack trudged wearily home, carrying his things, a mile and a half to his lonely, but peaceful, apartment. He thought he might just sleep away the rest of the day.

After quitting his job at the newspaper, life for Jack became empty days of TV and walking the streets He had built up quite a savings, but he knew his funds could soon get mighty low without a paying job. Things would have to change. He didn't feel good about just being lazy and not looking for another job. Still, he was having a hard time reconciling himself to all that was going wrong.

One day, as he was aimlessly walking, Jack stepped off the curb without looking and was almost clobbered by a huge garbage truck. A hand seemed to reach out and stop him. He wondered whether it was Shiny Man.

One of his walks took him past the pastor's church, but he decided not to go in. A few blocks further took him past the restaurant where he and Pastor Ed had eaten lunch together. No, he would not stop there either.

After thinking it over, Jack changed his mind and decided he would go back and get something to eat for he was hungry. He really hoped the pastor would be there. When he stepped inside and looked around, he was relieved to see that, sure enough, Pastor Ed was there.

Jack walked to the booth and was happy about the beat of his heart and the pastor's big smile on his face. "I'm so glad to see you, son," said Pastor Ed. His warm handshake made Jack glad he had changed his mind about coming in. "I was just getting ready to order. It's my turn to buy." A good meal was just what Jack needed. He had again been abusing his body by not eating the way he should.

"I have something I have been saving for you, Jack," said Pastor Ed. He held out a Bible, with print large enough to read without glasses, if a person needed them, yet small enough to put in his jacket pocket.

Jack accepted the Bible and offered more information: "I quit my job, and I've been pretty useless since I saw you last."

He felt comfortable with Pastor Ed again and discussed things that were happening in his life while idly flipping through the pages of the Bible. "Pastor, I don't think I want this—not right now." Jack was sorry to hurt the fellow's feelings. After all, he was a pastor and a really nice guy. Jack could see the disappointment on his face. "Keep it for me, will you—for a while?"

Jack's glass of water fell over. "How did that happen?" he asked. "I didn't even touch it."

Pastor Ed handed him some napkins. "Oh well, it was almost empty." No, thought Jack, "I hadn't even taken one drink out of it."

Jack didn't think that Bible was going to do him any good; he didn't want it lying around but didn't want to throw it away either.

"Pastor, can you see ... uh, feel ... uh. Does anything seem strange to you?"

Jack was taken back to the time he was drowning in his family's swimming pool. With all that had been going on in his life over the past couple of years, he hadn't thought a whole lot about Shiny Man. Now he was again feeling that presence.

Pastor Ed sensed Jack's uneasy tension. "Well, I do see lots of things and feel even more things. Think about this, Son: is the Lord speaking to you?"

Ignoring Pastor Ed's question, Jack said, "There's something I think I should tell you," Jack said. After a short hesitation, he continued. "I –ah--have this angel—uh, I mean angle—about this group of homeless people I saw—uh--I think I better go to the restroom. I'll be right back." He rushed down the aisle, bumping into someone.

When he returned to the booth he was sharing with Pastor Ed, he apologized with a broad grin. "Whew, it's not wise to wait so long when nature calls. I'll take the Bible, and thank you; I sure appreciate it."

Pastor Ed inwardly shook his head with confusion about Jack but was pleased he took the Bible. When they parted, Jack expressed thanks for the lunch and suggested they meet again in a couple weeks. Pastor Ed heartily agreed and turned his way and walked back to the church. There was a serious look on his face. His heart was puzzled about Jack. He would have a lot to discuss with his wife when he got home that evening.

Jack turned his way, carrying the Bible, which was burning his hand. He reproached himself, "Why did I have to open my mouth, giving Pastor Ed the impression I wanted a Bible?" Jack hadn't opened a Bible since leaving his parents' home to go to college. He found it bewildering that he hadn't even darkened the door of a chapel or a church since he had entered college. From the time he was little until college began, he had never objected going to church. In fact, he used to look forward to the services and to his involvement with the youth group. Regardless, he knew it wasn't going to kill him to get into the Bible a bit.

When Jack got back to his apartment, he tossed the Bible onto his bed. He decided he would look at it later. "Yes, later," he said. He felt a flick on his earlobe, and he grinned a secret smile. "Is Shiny Man teasing me?" He thought.

It was not very realistic, but it was a fascinating thought. He thought that maybe he would write a citizen's article about angels, for a spot in the newspaper. He went to the refrigerator for a soda, popped the top and took a swallow. Then making himself a sandwich, he picked up the Bible, and settled in his recliner. He sighed a happy sigh. As he did so, he thought he heard a soft chuckle.

CHAPTER 12

A Friend In Need

When Jack walked into the eatery two weeks later, he was glad to see that Pastor Ed was there. Almost tracing his steps of a couple weeks ago he walked back to the booth where Pastor Ed was sitting, grinned happily, and sat down across from him. Jack felt a flick on his other earlobe, and the saltshaker fell over.

"What? Oh, hello, Jack. I was just thinking about you. I haven't ordered yet; your timing is perfect. Hope things are better for you." Pastor Ed righted the saltshaker.

That special warm feeling just seemed to flow through Jack and over the whole room. He really liked this man. He seemed like a great friend. As Pastor Ed and Jack ate their meal, a camaraderie and mutual fellowship turned their conversation to what was going on in the church world.

"Ah, Pastor, the Bible you gave me, I have been reading it and have noticed Jesus' commands about things we're to do, and things like where He said, I call you friend. Does that mean all of us? Then he said we are to go unto the world and preach the gospel. That's a pretty big order. How do we do that?" Jack was full of questions, but those were the two main ones.

"These things concern me greatly, Jack, Pastor Ed said, as he lifted his shoulders in a shrug and smiled, so pleased that Jack was reading it. He felt the Holy Spirit was at work. "About being His friend, I'm sure not everybody feels comfortable with that, but I want to be His friend. About going unto all the world, you know that your world right now is right here where you are, just as my world is right here where I am, and here is where I'm working to do what the Lord has commanded. What's your take on those two things?"

With his elbow on the table and his chin on his hand, Jack fell into deep thought.

"Tell you what, Jack. I have an appointment in about five minutes. Let's think on these things and meet again in two weeks. Okay with you?

Jack stood and turned to him. "Oh sure, Pastor, and by the way, have you ever felt an angel close to you? Jack ducked his head and examined his left thumbnail. He decided it was all right and looked up, peering closely into the pastor's eyes.

"Well, we can talk about that later too." Jack had caught Pastor Ed's attention. He felt like a Holy Jolt of lightening had compressed him into a glowing ember. Jack didn't seem to notice anything different about Pastor Ed. They looked at one another, thinking about their next meeting with great anticipation. Pastor felt he was standing on a pleasant cloud. "Lord, what is it about this young man? Guide me, and my words to him. Use me but help me to keep my hands off while You do what You have in mind for him."

After shaking hands and waving good-bye, they went their own ways. Pastor Ed had a puzzled smile on his face as he walked back to the church. *An angel?* He thought. "Well, anything's possible with God!" Feeling a wild urge, he wanted to run back to Jack, grab him by the shoulders, and shake out of him what he meant by "an angel." Grinning at himself, he walked on to his duties at church.

Two weeks later, as the two friends met for lunch, the place was crowded; all the tables and booths were taken. Luckily two customers sitting at the counter had just finished eating and noticing Pastor Ed and Jack just coming in, motioned to them and pointed at their seats. Pastor Ed smiled and nodded. They had seats. As the two men stood to leave, Pastor Ed shook their hands and thanked them.

Pastor Ed was surprised but glad that they had the same waitress at the counter. She was almost like a good friend. He liked how she catered to him regarding the way he liked certain foods to be prepared and that she was aware of his usual, pressed time, so got his food to him a bit quicker.

Planning ahead, Pastor Ed had made sure he would have no appointment until later that afternoon. He wanted to talk about the two Scriptures Jack had read and was asking the two weeks before. When Jack mentioned reading Jesus' command about going unto all, the world, Pastor Ed had been instantly interested.

Meeting again, they went into Jack's questions and that took them into the deep discussion about street ministry. Pastor Ed shared his feelings about that issue "We are not a large church, and dealing with the homeless requires quite an investment in the form of money as well as manpower. Still, I feel it is something churches must deal with. You mentioned something about an angel; then you changed it to an angle about the homeless group you discovered under that overpass. Can you tell me more about that?"

Glad that Pastor Ed did not push the issue of an Angel, Jack explained some of his feelings, "I just somehow feel drawn to those fellows for some reason, Pastor. I feel a measure of concern to do something for them, but I don't know how to do anything or how to explain it. I have something in my heart for those men, but I can't get it straight in my mind." Jack ignored the issue of the angel.

"I'm well acquainted with that feeling, Jack. Now hang on, with what I'm about to say. Don't shut down on me, okay? I'm sure you know how much I would like for you to be a part of our church, but I won't pressure you. However, how about coming and getting involved with our street ministry, I have a feeling you might find answers to some of your questions. What do you think?"

Pastor Ed was hopeful but didn't want to be pushy with Jack. He saw the wall go up and was sorry about that. "I in no way want anything to interfere with our friendship, Jack. Just think about it. I will not pressure you in any way."

Jack smiled broadly. "Pastor, it feels like you just opened the door for me to come in. Yeah, I'll be there next Sunday—nine sharp." The wall was down. Pastor's heart soared and he felt like shouting thanks to God.

"You don't have a car, though, do you?"

"That won't be a problem. I walk around town all the time. I'm used to putting the miles on these shoes." Jack was getting into walking.

"We'll talk about your question about Jesus' command to go unto to all the world and about Jesus calling us a friend when we get together here the next time." Pastor Ed got the feeling that he was not to push but was to wait on Jack to bring up wanting more right then. For Jack, that sealed their next meeting. Nothing was going to spoil that communion between them.

After they sat for a few moments more, Jack shook his head several times. Pondering what he had said about the homeless group, he realized, with trepidation, what a weak Christian he was. More Scripture came to him: Trust in the Lord with all your heart. Lean not in your own understanding. In all your ways acknowledge Him and He will make your paths straight. (Proverbs 3:5-6)

Murmuring, to himself Jack said, "Lord, you can't be saying this, I'm so new at this." His thoughts were going ninety miles an hour. "Gosh, who do I think I am? I don't know enough to do anything for those homeless men!"

Pastor Ed heard his mumbled prayer. He reached out to Jack, laid a gentle hand on Jack's arm, and said, "As the Lord calls, He also equips." (Ephesians 4:11-12 And He gave some to be for the perfecting of the saints, for the work of ministry for the edifying of the body of Christ)

The tension went out of Jack's body, erasing what seemed to be a fear that would try to steal in and get a foothold.

"You will get a good testing as you work with the people at church when they go out to the streets. You'll know, Jack. God is not going to call you to something where He doesn't have His hand on you. Give it time, and put your trust in Him."

Pastor Ed knew very well what Jack was feeling. Sometimes it's scary to be called by the Lord.

The time was up; Pastor Ed had to get back to the church. He said to Jack, "We'll see you at church Sunday?" They shook hands on it, and stood up. Pastor Ed gave him a light hug around the shoulder.

Pastor Ed usually did a lot of thinking and meditating while he walked. As he walked back to the church that day, he was wondering and praying as he talked to the Almighty wondering, "Is Jack still back in his four-year-old level of understanding his relationship with the Lord? He has evidently gotten into John, chapter fifteen. Where is he spiritually?"

Still pondering, Pastor Ed wondered, "Does he think of Jesus as way out there somewhere? "If that is the case, I'm anxious for Jack to learn who Jesus wants to be to all of us. If Jack is called to minister to that group of people under the overpass, then he will positively need Jesus in him. He couldn't do it on his own. If he did try it on his own, the enemy would really have a heyday, with him and any unbelievers he talked to".

There was more Pastor Ed wanted to know about that interesting young man. The enormity of a possible call from God to his young friend caused a thundering in his being. Pastor Ed didn't know if it was from fear or from excitement.

He wouldn't push the issue but would be sensitive to whatever was in store for Jack. He didn't even know for sure if Jack was saved or not. "All in good time, Lord. Help me to follow your wishes, not mine."

Pastor Ed got the idea that Jack was thinking of going among the group of homeless people undercover, as a homeless person himself. The pastor was hopeful that Jack would return to the church regularly for prayer and council.

Deep in his heart, Pastor Ed wanted to be there if he could help in any way. Besides having Jack in his daily prayers he also wanted the Lord to be the one to put His hand on Jack, so Pastor Ed didn't push him. It was up to God to open the opportunity—or to hold back.

CHAPTER 13

The Good News

The eatery was getting to be their regular spiritual meeting, place. When they met two weeks later, it was significant in that as they talked, a big load was lifted from Jack's shoulders.

"Thanks, Pastor, for what you said to me our last meeting--about doing anything for the homeless men that I saw. For a minute there, I guess I was trying to steal God's glory."

"Oh, I don't believe that at all." Pastor Ed remembered some things about himself when he first started pastoring. "You know, every once in a while, I have to be reminded of who is doing what. The Lord always gives me a sweet rescue from myself as I repent of trying to steal His glory. He knows I don't really want to do that. If I begin to get all blown up about myself, He has a painless way of sticking a pin in my balloon. Then I remember how much He loves me, as much as—even more than—I love my son. Anyone, everyone, has to remember, whenever you do anything in the Lord's name, you are only a tool, Jack—a tool in the Lord's hands."

After letting that sink into Jack's spirit, Pastor Ed continued. "If anyone should feel a call to work in the Lord's field of lost people, our part is to say yes or no. I would not push anyone either way in that manner of things. If you say no, the Lord will find someone else. If you are thinking about saying yes, pray about it. Don't rush into it; give it time. We will help you to study to show yourself approved." (2nd Timothy 2:15)

Reiterating what he had already said, he stressed his next words. "If you still want to give it a go, evidently the Lord feels you could handle being His tool. Remember, too, that a tool is, in the sense that we think of a good old-fashioned hammer or screwdriver, used by the skilled artisan. It doesn't get up off of the bench and work on its own. The master who has a hold of it--guides it."

Pastor Ed had to smile as he told Jack of a humorous incident. "I don't know that this has anything to do with what we have been talking about but I'm reminded of an incident with my young son. I was sitting out on our back patio, reading and my son, Jeff, was playing with a neighbor friend. I heard Jeff bragging that he had the best swimming pool of everyone. I put down my book and walked over to them. Laying my hand on Jeff's shoulder, I asked him, 'Who bought this pool, Jeff?' It took a moment for him to realize what I was referring to.

"He shrugged his shoulder, carefully shaking my hand off, and said, 'We did, Dad.' I had to make my point here, so I emphasized it: '*Who* bought it?'

"He got it. He shrugged again, sheepishly grinned, and said, 'You did, Dad'.

Pastor Ed continued, "I gave him a small hug and stopped him from moving away. His neighbor friend was paying close attention now. I softly put my hand on his shoulder again and asked, as I lifted his face to me so he could see I was smiling with lifted eyebrows. And who gave me the money to buy it? I asked."

"A frown crossed his little brow, as he felt confused, and then a great smile altered his whole body. 'Well, God did,' he said. Then he added something he had memorized: 'All things come from You, oh Lord'!" Pastor Ed had to chuckle and smiled big, he went on,

"Now it was time for the neighbor boy to pull back his head with a serious look and raised eyebrows. Out of his mouth came one word: 'Yeah.'

"I tried not to laugh out loud, but I gave him a pat on the shoulder too. I told them, "You fellows have a short time for a good swim before supper; go for it!"

Pastor Ed added the rest, "Later, while we were eating, Jeff stopped with his fork halfway to his mouth. 'You know what, Dad?' he said. 'It is hard to always remember that everything does come from God, even storms, but when bad things happen to us, it's mostly our own fault or because of someone else.' "He started to move the fork toward his mouth again but stopped short, "Or because we mess up, huh, Dad? Remember when I lost my ball glove. God didn't do that; I just forgot to pick it up when I left the park, and when we went back it was gone.' "I felt proud of my son for his understanding"

Jack, then had to chuckle. Pastor Ed had a good way of helping a guy out of a corner.

Time enough had passed in their next two weeks for the two friends to think about things that had passed between them the last time they were together. Pastor Ed and Jack were waiting for their lunch, sitting at the counter again because all the tables and booths were full. Business was picking up for Pastor Ed's favorite eating-place. It was different sitting at the counter rather than a booth, but they could still talk.

Happy to have the same waitress working at the counter, they didn't have to wait long for their food. Everything was to their liking when she put their plates before them. Jack could hardly wait for the blessing from Pastor Ed. He was hungry and almost attacked his food. Halfway through he sat back, partially satiated, almost embarrassed by his manners. Pastor Ed was seriously wondering if

Jack was running out of money. The crowd was clearing out, so, the two of them didn't feel rushed to finish their food. He had to smile as Jack was almost finished and was ready for some answers about the questions that had piqued his interest.

"Pastor, you know where Jesus tells the fellows who follow him around, 'I call you friends'—does that mean all of us? I bet you are a friend of Jesus, right?"

"Thanks, Jack. Yes I am, and I'm glad it shows." Pastor Ed knew what Jack had on his mind. He smiled to himself, happy about Jack's persistence for answers—for his seeking from his readings.

He was ready to clarify. "Well, Jesus said "You are my friends, if you do whatsoever I command you." If we do what He commands, He calls us friends. (John 15:14-15) It also says that Abraham believed God and was counted as a friend of God. (Isaiah 41:8)

He referred to several people as friends; for example, He said, "Our friend, Lazarus sleepeth." (John 11:11) I feel like I'm a friend of God; how do you feel, Jack?"

A pleasant, faraway look came over Jack's face, and his eyes became shiny with unshed tears, "I would like for Him to call me His friend."

Pastor Ed felt the Holy Spirit guiding him as he laid a hand on Jack's shoulder. "You know, it also says, 'You must be born again.' Have you been born again, Jack?"

Jack sat with his mouth almost open; he hesitated. A tear spilled over as he answered. "Would I know it if I were, Pastor?"

Nodding his head slightly, Pastor Ed said, "Yeah, I believe you would. Would you like to know for sure, Jack?"

"Yeah! How do I do that? What do I have to do?"

The waitress standing behind the counter piped up and said, "Yeah, I would too."

The young fellow sitting to the right of Jack joined in. "Yeah, me too, Pastor."

Because he was so riveted to what they were talking about, Jack wasn't paying attention to the two people near him.

Pastor Ed went on, saying, "Let's go to the Bible you're reading. Do you have it in your pocket, Jack?"

"Sorry, Pastor, I left it at home."

"Well, that's okay. In the Book of Romans it tells us, 'All have sinned. (Romans 3: 23 KJV) Some people sin by thoughts, some by words, and even some in deeds. Some people maybe don't sin quite as much as others—some maybe a whole lot more—but sin is sin regardless of the measure we may want to put on it. Just remember this, God's Word, the Bible, says we have *all* fallen short of God's desires—of His great glory—so we have to be forgiven for those sins."

Jack said, "Yeah, well I remember a bad one. I didn't do it, but I wanted to beat up the guy that was standing there with my fiancée when she broke up with me. I wanted to mash his face to a pulp."

The waitress looked down sorrowfully and slowly nodded.

Likewise, the young fellow beside Jack looked away, saying, "Boy, do I ever know how you feel."

Pastor Ed didn't comment on the confessions being made but continued. "Our sins make our Father in heaven feel sorrowful because, as the Bible says, He can't look upon sin. If we feel badly— if we regret having sinned—we are to tell Him we're sorry; it's called repentance. We have to confess; we have to tell Him about our sins. It says in Romans 10:9-10 that we are to confess with our mouth, all of the sins we can remember. Since He is God, He already knows what we have done anyway, but it says we are to confess with our mouth, and then ask Him to forgive us and to come live in us—live in our hearts.

It's sort of like apologizing to your mom if you broke something she really liked through carelessness or anger. She might already know you did it, but she will feel better about you if you tell her you did it, that you feel bad about what ever you did, and that you're sorry.

"Well, if I do that now, will I be born again?" Jack asked with wonder on his face, sincerely wanting to know, still not paying attention to the other two young people.

"Yeah, is that all right, or do we have to go to church or something?" the young fellow asked.

"If I wait, my boyfriend might talk me out of it," said the shy waitress.

"No, you can do it right now, right here," said Pastor Ed. Looking at each of them he asked, "Do you want to do that? They nodded and said yes. Pastor Ed turned to the cook who Pastor Ed noticed was paying close attention, tears were running down his chubby cheeks and asked him if he would like that. He wiped his tears away and nodded his head vigorously.

Pastor Ed, with great joy, led those four, precious young people in the sinner's prayer, covering what he had explained to them. They repeated each sentence, and at the end they together said, "Amen." It is hard to believe, but only then did Jack become consciously aware of the others. Smiling with exuberance, he jumped up and began pumping their hands, shouting with gusto. "Wow! This is, like, really great! We're going walk the streets of heaven together. Pastor, You're never getting rid of us."

Grabbing the opportunity to seal them to Christ, by their understanding of what had just happened to them Pastor Ed, almost shouting too. "Let's have a celebration—a party, no less. Would that be fun? You are Christians now, and Christians like to have fun!"

(John 3:33 He that has received his testimony has set to his seal that God is true) (Ephesians 1-13 In whom you also trusted...you were sealed with that Holy Spirit of promise.)

"Where shall we meet?" asked Jack.

"Don't you have a church, Pastor? The young fellow next to Jack wondered.

"Sure do, and it's only two-blocks down here on Twenty-Fourth Street. Does anyone need a ride? No? I'll see you all tomorrow evening at seven then. I'll have the side door open and be outside waiting so you won't get lost, and I'm treating. Does everyone like soda, hotdogs, and chips?" Everyone answered with big smiles.

"Could I bring my guitar?" asked the cook as he joined them. Pastor Ed heartily agreed to that suggestion

"If either of you wish to bring someone with you—a parent, brother or sister, boyfriend or girlfriend—that will be fine," said Pastor Ed. "We'll have a real party and do some singing."

All four of the people who were saved that day in the restaurant started going regularly to Pastor Ed's church and began to come to a deep understanding and to feel at home. They were touched with the member's friendliness, as Jack was that first day he met many coming out of the Church. Through Pastor Ed's teaching and group prayers they came into the joy and close relationship with the Lord.

CHAPTER 14

A New Commitment

Although Jack's life would have been considered Clean Living he wished he had started sooner with helping in the street ministry. He hadn't really *known* the Lord. He only knew *about* Him. He knew about the President, but he didn't Know him. Having a knowledge and relationship with the Lord, his life took on a richer and different meaning. He was not thinking only of himself. Jesus' new commandment to love one another took on a deeper meaning—to help make peoples' lives better in Christ.

(John 13: 34-35; A new commandment I give unto you, that you love one another; as I have loved you, that you also love one another. By this shall all men know that you are my disciples, if you have love one to another.)

Jack wondered how he could do that. He started by getting involved in the street ministry, and it wasn't as threatening as he thought it would be. He didn't have to do or say anything at first; he just observed. In participating with the street ministry, Jack remembered having been on many of the same streets where they went, from his time at his newspaper job. He remembered a few of the people too. Some seemed to just hang together and reinforce one another in their doings and beliefs.

There was one fellow who was a mystery to him. He seemed to be a loner--he fascinated Jack. He just didn't seem to belong there. Every once in a while he would catch the fellow with his eye on him and the man would then turn away. He seemed to be interested in Jack, maybe because Jack did not approach or talk to any of the people—not yet anyway. Jack was learning; he was feeling more comfortable and caring about the people's many different circumstances. He felt pretty good when he got promoted to handing out the sandwiches. That was pleasant. He got to shake hands with more and more of the people and would sometimes give him a smile.

He was glad he had left the newspaper job, for he was investing a surprising amount of time and dedication at the church in their street ministry. Jack felt drawn to this new work. After some concentrated work, the church elders, with the recommendation from the pastor, offered Jack a position on the church staff, that of Directing street ministry. With a lot of soul searching and gathering necessary knowledge, Jack became more familiar and understanding of the plights and individual differences of street people.

He was devouring his Bible and learning more of what life was really all about in the Christian world. He felt he understood Jesus' new commandment better and to have a deeper understanding of what it meant; We are here to love one another, making the world a better place in which to live; and loving them meant treating them as Christ treats us, making their life better in any way that came up in which he was able to do.

There was one team member, a young lady, named Fleeta, whom Jack found himself working with almost consistently. She was a part of the street ministry and had volunteered for secretarial work, which took a lot of the work off his shoulders. She was a hard worker, almost to the point of working too hard.

Several times he found her crying alone somewhere. She just brushed it off, saying, "Yes, I have to admit I am working too hard." She was an appealing, almost pathetic, childlike girl, yet wise and angelic. He told her she needed to go have some fun.

She gave a cute smile. "I don't have anyone to have fun with, Jack."

"Well, you have me. I'll take you to dinner right after we quit work. How's that?"

Fleeta froze in the middle of pouring a glass of iced tea for them, staring at Jack in disbelief. "Oh, I … uh …I … oh, Jack."

"Well, what do you say?" He took the glass from her hand, fearing she would drop it.

Laughing and crying all at the same time, she threw her arms around his neck, throwing him off balance. To keep from being bowled over, he had to grab her around the waist, and they staggered around and around to keep from falling as he set the glass on the counter.

"Whoa, I didn't mean to startle the life out of you."

"Hey, are you two engaged?" Tony, one of the workers in the street ministry, was standing in the doorway.

He was really teasing, but Jack looked down at Fleeta. This girl had completely changed since helping him out at church, and he had grown quite fond of her. He didn't pine over the loss of Jill when he and Fleeta were working together. He felt he knew her pretty well and was surprised at how good it felt to have his arms around her waist. She was muscular, yet so soft. She had been a comfort to him. And she smelled good—so fresh. He had thought a couple times, it would be nice to touch her shiny dark hair to see if it was as soft as it looked. For that reason, he had purposely kept a distance from her, yet here she was in his arms.

"Well, yes … I mean, no, but we will soon be. Fleeta, will you marry me? He loosed his arms from around her waist and had slipped down on one knee. "I don't have a ring to give you yet, but will you—will you marry me?"

"Oh Jack! Oh yes! I think I'm going to—" And faint she did!

"Tony get a cold, wet cloth, quick. Hurry!" Jack was frantic.

"Jack and Jack are going to get married, help! Get some water; she fainted!" Tony ran down the hall and into the fellowship hall, screaming at the top of his lungs.

"Tony, for heaven's sake, who did you say were going to get married?" asked the church secretary.

"I said Fleeta and Fleeta … I mean Jack and Jack … I mean Jack and Fleeta are going to get engaged. I mean they are engaged—just now—and she fainted!"

It didn't take long for a crowd to gather around the prostrate girl and Jack. As Fleeta began to revive, Jack picked her up in his arms and carried her to a sofa in the fellowship hall.

"Someone call a doctor, quick!" Jack was beside himself. "Hurry." He was beside himself.

"I think she's coming around, Jack; let's wait. Tell us what happened." Someone at his elbow suggested.

"I asked her to marry me, and she fainted!" Jack offered through his befuddlement.

Shakily reaching her hand out, Fleeta tried to sit up, and many hands were trying to help her. She reached for Jack.

"I'm s-s-so sorry, Jack. Everybody, I'm sorry. I feel better. Where is Pastor Ed? Is he b-busy?"

Good ole Tony had already gone and knocked on Pastor Ed's door. Pastor Ed didn't have anyone in his office, so Tony was quick to deliver the lowdown on all that had transpired, getting it straight that time. Pastor Ed was soon on the way to where the excitement was happening—in the fellowship hall. Tony felt important to be of some help.

Mrs. Townson, Pastor Ed's secretary, relayed what had happened, and everyone began to return, each to his own duties. Seeing everyone had left but for Pastor Ed and Jack, Fleeta held out her hand to Pastor Ed and pleaded with him.

"Pastor, I need to talk to you."

Here was a bigger problem than he was ready to deal with-- right there.

"Jack, is there anything urgent you need to do right now?

"Well, we were all about to go out to the street. People will be expecting us. I don't know if we should cancel," pondered Jack as he looked questioning, at Pastor Ed.

"Don't cancel. Go, Jack. I am all right now. I will just stay here and rest. Go, please, go. Okay?" Fleeta spoke up and answered for Pastor Ed.

Pastor Ed decided that was a good idea. "Go ahead, Jack; She will be all right."

Jack gathered the needed materials, gathered the group of workers, and touched Fleeta on the cheek. "We'll be back as soon as we can. Bye, bye. Are you sure you're all right?" She nodded to assure him, and he and the workers left.

As soon as they were gone, Fleeta stared at Pastor Ed. "Pastor, I can't marry him, no way—you know why."

"Shall we give it some time? We'll seek the Lord and see what He has in mind. What do you think of that? He is pretty smart, you know." Pastor waited for her answer.

Looking at him with understanding, Fleeta agreed. "Yes, that will be a good idea. I'd like to go home now and rest. I don't live very far. I'll be all right in a few minutes. I never in my life expected anyone as fine as Jack would ever propose to me.

"Fleeta, you are a fine Christian and a fine person."

"I so wish I could believe that."

"Remember, Fleeta, you are not responsible for other people's sins—just like I'm not responsible for all of the sins of my congregation.

I'm here to love them and guide them, as they will permit me to. They must look to Jesus to be restored. He restores our soul and leads us into righteousness for His blessed Name's sake in so many different ways. And who is the Lord?"

"I remember, Pastor. He is my shepherd—Psalm twenty-three."

"Right, and what does he do for each one of us?"

Gaining strength and sitting up, with tears in her eyes and a smile on her face, she said, "He leads us into paths of righteousness. He restores us. No matter what others do to us, Jesus restores our soul. Thanks for reminding me again, Pastor."

"Yes, and would you like to talk again tomorrow?"

"That will be fine. Thank you again, Pastor. You help make me feel okay about myself."

"That is the Lord's Word that does that for us. Keep His Word in your heart. Remember, we are precious in His sight. See you at one o'clock, tomorrow."

Fleeta walked out into the fresh air with her shoulders back, her head up, and contentment in her heart. It felt good to love the Lord—she was engaged to wonderful Jack Hampstan.

When the team returned from their ministry with the street people, Jack asked Pastor Ed, "What is all the commotion in the street? What happened?" Pastor Ed took Jack into his office immediately upon his return. He had sad news to relate to him.

"Pray with me for a moment." They took each other's hand as Pastor Ed prayed, "Merciful and all knowing Lord, who gives Your strength, Your help to all Your children, Please give us Your strength now, we pray in Jesus Holy Name. Amen." Jack felt Pastor Ed's hand tremble and could see he was visually dazed as he tried to hold on to himself. He continued, "It was Fleeta, Jack. She wanted to go home—a car hit her—the Lord took her home with Him, Son. I believe this is the hardest thing I have ever had to tell someone." Jack stared, took a deep breath, put his hands on Pastor

Ed's shoulder and began to weep. The two friends supported one another for a time.

"This-uh-this can't—tell me--what you can, Pastor."

"After you left, Jack, she sat up and we chatted as she gained her strength. I gave her a donut to eat and glass of milk to drink. She wanted to go home to rest—I can hardly believe this happened—I can only believe, that it was her time. It occurred only a short time after you and your team left--she just glowed, Jack, she was so happy that you had proposed."

Pastor shook his head in disbelief of what he was relaying to his young friend.

"Jack, Officer O'Conner explained to me, officials found no address to send the report of the accident to. Knowing that she was a member of our congregation, they almost immediately sent this to me."

Pastor Ed handed the report to Jack to look over, Pastor further explained to Jack, how his good friend, Officer O'Conner, sat with him and relayed what he had seen and heard from people on the scene.

Jack was so torn up he didn't want to know about it, yet, he found himself wanting every detail so he could almost be with her. "Tell me Pastor—I have nothing of her–only some memories—tell me everything, please."

"Here is what Officer O'Conner told me, Jack: Witnesses revealed that a car with three noisy, young boys, who had thrown empty beer cans out the window, came careening around the corner, going way over the speed limit as they hit her. Some commented that the boys seemed to feel they owned the world—they finally stopped and came back to look at the girl. Others agreed, they were going so fast, there was, no way, the driver could have stopped for the young girl crossing the street—they said the crossing sign was in her favor.

Two witnesses, on the other corner of the street said they themselves, had just barely gotten out of the way as the car almost ran upon the curb. They said that then the driver jerked the car real short and the car was back and forth, halfway on the wrong side of the street and then back. When asked if she screamed, they said, "No, it happened so fast she didn't even see them coming at her."

One young couple that was questioned said, "We are a neighbor of that driver, and it is his habit of driving reckless and too fast. He has been stopped before, right on our street for driving too fast. He worries his poor mother with his drinking. She's had a lot of trouble with him being disobedient and unruly."

The officer delivering the report to Pastor Ed told him, when they questioned the fellow driving, he said, " I yelled at her, "You'd better get out of our way," The kid driving thought for a moment, then he yelled, "Dang, she didn't move fast enough".

Pastor Ed told Jack, "Officer O'Conner had put a comforting hand on my shoulder as he was telling me all of this and, Jack, he even prayed for me while I was trying to listen to him. I had never known Officer O'Conner to even respect prayer. Officer O'Conner expressed a belief in Jesus being able to make a difference and ended in Jesus name as I had done with him several times. I feel Jesus heard the man, the way he prayed in faith for me, I'm sure the Lord bathed him, as he prayed for me, with the Holy Spirit."

Throwing his own arms around himself, Jack gasped, "That's amazing, Pastor. Do you think anything good could have possibly, in anyway, come from this—anything? I'm so mixed up Pastor, I can't get my thoughts or words straight."

"I don't know for sure yet, Jack, but in the past, Officer O'Conner usually resisted and shied away from my talking about the Lord. I'd like to believe, the way he prayed for me in my falling apart in front of him, that the Lord dealt with him at that moment of my need.

"Did he say anything more about the accident, Pastor?" Jack asked, as he put his hand on his friend's shoulder, beginning to realize the impact the news had on Pastor Ed.

"Officer O'Conner said she was DOA, when the ambulance pulled up to the hospital and, Jack, there were tears in the man's eyes as he told me."

Jack and Pastor Ed, both wept as Pastor told Jack of her life: "Her father had sold his daughter repeatedly for a bottle of whisky or a six-pack of beer. We got her out of his house and into an apartment of her own. After she left, he killed himself with all the alcohol he had stored up. She was a tormented girl, son. It's too bad the accident took her life. She was beginning to have a new life. She had received Jesus as her Savior. God has her safe in his arms now. She is at peace." The event shook them both to the core.

"Jack, my friend, I really do believe this is one of the hardest things I have ever had to tell anyone." The news shook Pastor Ed and seemed to age him.

Jack was unable to think. He felt bewildered and confused. "I'm just dumbfounded, Pastor Ed, I can't believe she's gone."

Pastor filed the report away for Jack to look at later, if he wished to read it in detail, but he was sure it would not be read by him. He thought to himself, "God knows what is best for each of us, though it is so hard for us to understand at times. In my heart I believe Jill is just a whisper from being found."

Pastor faced the hard understanding that the great gift of Free Will is given to each person, even those boys who had killed Fleeta. He accepted the fact of Jesus' gift, Free will is given to everyone at birth but realized too about 1Peter 5:8; be sober, be vigilant; because your adversary, the devil as a roaring lion, walks about, seeking whom he may devour.

It was going to be hard for Pastor Ed to break the news to his wife. She had met and loved the young girl. His wife ministered to

Fleeta and became her friend. They had become attached to her. They both felt Fleeta had been, finally, freed of the hold the father had over her; that she no longer had to obey him. His wife had been thinking of adopting her into their home, loving her as a daughter.

Jack and Pastor Ed took a fishing trip together at a log cabin in the country owned by a member of the church. They both ministered to one another in their sorrows. Pastor Ed had counseled the abused girl. She had come a long way but had quite a way to go to be able to separate from the way she had been treated, to realizing she was the worthwhile person, to the real goodness, that she truly was. She was beginning to realize that she had access to the joy of the Lord's gift of decent life. Jack recognized the gift that was in her, though he had been unaware of how her father, who had been assigned to love her and care for her wellbeing, had robbed her of the beauty the Lord had in store for her life. She had been on the way to receiving it back.

In due time while they there in the wide-open spaces, Pastor Ed and Jack devised a plan. It excited them both, but it would take a lot of prayer and time to work it out. Pastor had a lady in his congregation who worked with abused persons. He would like to see it funded and grow to make a difference in many lives—like Fleeta's.

CHAPTER 15

The Cup Runneth Over

Pastor Ed and Jack returned to the church and their duties. Jack buried himself in the street ministry, helping to bring many to the Lord and to a better life.

Several days later, Jack and Pastor Ed were at the ole eatery. They were enjoying their lunches more each time, but because of news that Pastor Ed had to share with Jack that day—news which had been delivered to him some days before—he had set aside several hours of time for this lunch hour. It was a pretty big thing to put on Jack. Pastor Ed could see Jack had something pressing to discuss with him but stopped him from going on. "I have another surprise for you, Jack, and no, it isn't another Bible!" His smile was wide and mysterious.

Wondering if he was going to like this news, Jack tried to be patient and hold the idea he wanted to discuss with Pastor Ed–he waited.

"I feel like I should go slow with this and give you time to brace yourself, but I'm going to blast it right out to you, my friend. An anonymous person has passed away, and he included the church for the larger part of his estate."

"Hey, that is great," said Jack. He lifted his coffee cup for a happy gesture of a toast.

Pastor Ed sat smiling, saying no more for a few moments, just looking at Jack with a lighthearted smirk, a couple wiggles of his eyebrows and a teasing manner.

"So?" said Jack.

"He named you in his will, son. He was impressed with you and the work you have been doing"

"Oh, no. Who would want to leave me anything in their will? What is it—maybe his dog?"

"He has left you five hundred thousand dollars."

Jack was speechless. He was dumbstruck. He had no words to express his understanding of what Pastor Ed had just told him. He held onto the edge of the table they sitting at. The room swam in front of him. He could mutter only one word: "Why?" He was bereft of any more speech.

"This gentleman was an only child, of an only child, of an only child. He had no relations left, but he did have a son—another only child. That son was killed three years ago in an automobile accident. The man admired you, and you reminded him of his son. He said he felt toward you in a fatherly way. Too bad he didn't make himself known to you, but he traveled quite a lot. He admired the work you have been doing for the Lord in the church. I never told him anything about your interest in the homeless group you came across. I didn't think it was my place to tell anyone."

"Could I just give it to the church? I don't need that much money."

"Son, I advise you to just put it in your bank and perhaps let it rest there for a time. I have a good feeling that you may need it in the future."

That was wise counsel.

"You are working with the street people pretty consistently, so do you still believe God has called you to that work?" asked Pastor Ed.

"I have to confess that I have been feeling restless doing that of late. I love the people, but like I said, I do feel—well, restless."

"Anything at all? Is God talking to you?"

Shaking his head in more confusion, Jack stared at his plate. Then a light turned on. His face seemed to glow as if sunshine had broken lose inside him. Jack's face lit up with the brightest smile. "How strange. When I looked at my plate full of food, I plainly saw in my mind that group of homeless people under that overpass. That's where I belong, Pastor—there, with those people. I don't want that money."

"We'll let the money business ride for a time, okay?" Pastor Ed smiled and looked down at his plate and softly said, "Thank You, Lord; those whom You call, You equip." He could plainly see there was going to be a need for more intense training for Jack.

Later there was a solemn, sincere service, at the church. Jack was dedicated to service to the Lord. He felt confident and sure that he was doing what God wanted him to do.

The garb Jack wore was amazingly authentic. It was tattered and torn, it even looked dirty, and it hung on him like a gunnysack. Looking at it, one might swear it would be smelly too. His bedroll was tied with a frayed piece of rope that matched his outfit. But there was a difference, perhaps. The worn quilt that held all the possessions he would have, had a secret pocket with his cell phone in it. The phone was set to vibrate when calls came in so the sound of a ring wouldn't give away its presence. There were two new batteries in another pocket as well. Other places had lumpy parts, typical of an old quilt that has become lumpy with use. Jack had let his beard grow, without trimming it. That, too, matched his badly worn hat and his flyaway hair that needed the care of a barber. It might be said that Jack had taken a course called "Days and Nights of the Homeless".

With the end of the lease on his little apartment and all evidence removed of his having been there, Jack turned in the key to the landlord. He was homeless, not friendless. Pastor Ed set it up for him to sleep on one of the pews in the church for that night and that night only. Pastor Ed treated him to breakfast the next morning at a place away from their usual one, so Jack ended up with a full belly, three crumpled one-dollar bills, and some small change.

Life was about to present some major challenges to this willing, new laborer, in his new vocation.

Trying not to stare, customers at the cash register waited as the man, obviously a pastor, paid for the food he had treated the dirty street guy to. Jack, also trying not to stare, clearly understood the diverse emotions expressed on the faces of those nearby. Realizing he was blushing, he felt some uncomfortable emotions: embarrassment, shame, resentment, and even anger. He wanted to rescue himself by explaining what he was about to do.

Jack dropped his eyes and looked at the floor. He was getting mad and wanted to punch each one of them for looking at him in such a way. Trying to come to terms with the momentary confusion going on inside of him, he slowly made his way nearer to the door.

For just a fleeting moment, he saw the different understandings of those present and was transported, transplanted, into a revolting, repulsive, unwanted part of society. A part of him wanted to turn and address those viewing him as such. He fought the desire to go back and explain what he was about, to tell them that this was not the true him. He wanted to tell them he was a noble, worthy, and responsible citizen—that he was a part of the same society that they were part of. He momentarily wanted to turn and plead with them to let him shed his exterior and reveal the real Jack: a college graduate, a man with a bank account, and a Christian—a part of the better society.

Feeling a hand on his shoulder, Jack looked to see who the kind person was, but there was no one near him. Everyone was treating him with disdain.

Then someone with pale sympathy, trying to get out the door was giving him space—a wide berth to get around him. Jack tried to move out of the way as much as he possibly could. He heard a voice say, "They treated me like this too."

Having witnessed all of this with a heavy heart, Pastor Ed caught up with Jack and waited for him while he opened the door. As he saw Jack's face and his eyes, understanding rolled over him.

Putting his arm lightly around Jack's shoulder, he felt Jack slightly withdraw. Pastor Ed had seen and experienced the hearts of many vagrants. He eased Jack out the door and they walked; they walked the walk of the broken ones.

CHAPTER 16

Different Introductions

With the heat of the late August sun on his shoulders, Jack removed his shabby jacket. Knowing he still had a good walk ahead of him before he got to the place where he had seen the group of homeless people, he pressed on. He was glad Pastor Ed had taken him to a restaurant at the edge of town. Anxiety gripped him as a thought hit him, "They might not even be there anymore. Then what?"

Jack had been walking for some hours, and the ache in his shoulder was getting more intense. He wondered if perhaps he'd put too much in his bedroll. Chewing on one of the good-sized apples and one of the good-sized nutrition bars that Pastor Ed had picked up for him, he determined he would walk until suppertime. Later, still walking, he mused about what his "supper" would be like: a repeat of another nutrition bar and apple, most likely. When he came to a large shade tree along the side of the road, he was more than willing to hide behind it and catch a few winks. What he found was almost too good to be true. There was a patch of long grass near the tree that was almost like a soft mattress. This was the life. With his head on his bedroll, he was soon fast asleep.

A soft nuzzling on his cheek stirred him. Opening his weary eyes, he found a large dog standing over him, wagging his tail. A paw on his shoulder brought him fully awake with a smile on his face Rolling over, though, he felt he could sleep some more. He heard a gun blast a ways off, and he opened his eyes to find the sun had come up.

Another gun blast brought him to his feet. A man coming closer started yelling at him, "Get out of here you lazy bum! Go get a job and you won't have to steal sleep in my field!" Another shot kicked up dirt close to his feet.

He grabbed his bedroll and high-tailed it down the road at a run with the dog running along with him. Cursing at the top of his lungs, the man yelled at the dog, "Dan, get back here! Dan! Come here, you no-good hound."

Not liking the situation, Jack yelled at the dog. "Git! Go away!" He stopped and pointed back as he yelled again. "Go! *Stay!*" Confused, the dog started back to the man. In a few seconds, Jack heard a loud yelp from the dog.

Jack did not like what he heard. It made him want to turn back, but the dog was not his, and he knew there was nothing he could do for him. Jack continued his retreat around a curve and down a hill, hoping it would take him out of sight of the man and his dog.

Facing the new day, Jack knew he had to find a safe place to stop where he could satisfy the grumbling in his midsection. The sun overhead, surprisingly, told him he had slept ten hours. Having forgotten to eat late yesterday before sleeping caused his stomach to complain. After he trudged along for another several hours, his heart leaped. There was the overpass. Would they remember him? Would they even still be there?

Jack's legs started trembling. The trembling brought him to his knees though he knew not whether it was from fatigue or fear. A welcome Scripture came to him: "Fear not, for I am with you" (Isaiah 41:10). "Thank You Lord." said Jack.

He was so exhausted that tears started pouring down his cheeks, and he remembered his mother giving him a confusing Scripture: "Give thanks always for all things." She had rubbed his little shoulder as she smiled and said, "Remember, it's *E P*, not *E T*, and you are five, and your brother is ten years older than you, so add five years to that and you come up with Ephesians five, verse twenty." So Jack heartily gave thanks that he was finally at his destination. With a wringing of loneliness in his heart, he remembered saying to his mother, "Gee, Mom, that's like a secret code!"

He never forgot that secret code. Yes, he needed to go see his parents again very soon. He sat down in the grass alongside the road and wiped away the tears and tried to calm himself. He couldn't go into their camp as he was. What would they think of a bawling grown man?

Looking around at the scenery, Jack noticed a cornfield just below him. At the edge of the cornfield, he noticed someone picking a young ear of corn. Oh, boy! If he got caught near that guy, he could find himself in trouble too, but he was too tired to move. He watched the man pull the husk from the ear of corn and was surprised to see him stuff the husk into his pocket. That seemed strange to Jack. What was he going to do, eat the husk later? The man looked up and motioned for Jack to come on down. Jack wondered whether the smile on his face was genuine or a trap. As Jack tried to get up, he stared at the man coming toward him. Too tired to run anymore, Jack just sat there. The fellow carefully pulled another ear of the young corn and kept coming. Jack gave up and lay back on his bedroll. The guy came near, and he sat on his haunches when he reached Jack. He then handed Jack the extra ear and just kept eating his.

"Where ya from, pard? Ya sure look tuckered out."

Jack tried his drawl. "From town. Sure no generous folk like you there."

"When did ya last eat,?" the guy asked,

"I don't remember."

The man took the ear of corn he had given Jack and pulled off the husk. He stuck that also in his other pocket.

"Why did you do that?" asked Jack, pointing to the husk in his pocket.

"You don't want to leave 'em on the ground 'cause the farmer knows what someone's done and he keeps an eye out. God made these to be et, and with the big field of 'em he's got, he knows he wants to contribet to the good a mankind. Eat up, pard. It'll jes go ta waste if ya don't." His one messy hand held the ear of corn as he stuck out the other. "Glad to meetcha, pard."

"Name's J. H.," said Jack.

"Name's Sid."

"Glad to meet you, Sid."

Jack was pleasantly surprised at how good the young field corn tasted. His conscience was sadly challenged, but he couldn't let that good ear of corn go to waste.

"Got any smokes?" asked Sid.

"Naw, I quit; it bothered my lungs."

"Wal, you jes smoked too much. My Pa use' ta say ya have ta use mo-der-ay-shun. I ony smoke the butts I find. I'll go grab a couple ears for the stew tonight. See ya down below."

Jack picked up his bedroll and started for the underpass. He hoped he understood what the guy meant by "see you down below." He slowly meandered to the concrete guardrail. Unexpectedly, Sid appeared below, near the overpass and pointed to the embankment, motioning for Jack to come down.

Butterflies in his stomach accompanied him as he came to stand beside Sid. He wondered whether any of them would recognize him. He was trusting in the Lord, and he hoped the beard and scraggly long hair would help. "Look at the sorry dude I found passed out 'longside the road," Sid said to a group of sorry-looking men. "Pard, this is the a-so-ce-ay-shun."

Some came and looked him over, a couple shook his hand, and one of them gave him a quick frisking. There was one little old lady. She sat where she was, looking him over as she twirled a thin strand of grey hair. Her mouth was drawn in a tight, thin line, but there was something interesting in her eyes. Jack wondered if she recognized him.

Sid pulled the husks off the corn he had gathered and threw them, along with the ones in his pockets, into a barrel in which a healthy fire was burning. He then chopped the corn into pieces, cob and all, and threw it all into a pot that was bubbling away. It smelled so wonderful. Jack's belly told him it would be a welcome feast.

Very soon, everyone was digging out eating utensils. Jack stood mesmerized, watching all sorts of vegetables roll around in the stew. There was a huge dipper that they used to serve themselves. With it they were each pulling amazing pieces of food from that pot. Two of the guys grabbed for the dipper at the same time. They started shoving and they began charging one another as though they were going to fight. Another man close by grabbed the dipper, stood back, and watched the scrappers. They rolled on the ground and finally stood up laughing. Those guys were just clowning. They were finding fun even at the food pot. Others grinned, shook their heads, and went on calmly dipping food onto their plates.

The last one in line dipped up the stew onto two plates. Jack figured the second plate was for him. Instead the man took it over to the little old lady. When he came back to the pot, he glanced at Jack and said, "Pard, we don't wait on no one 'cept Little Ma. If'n ya wanna eat, you hafta serve yerself."

Jack's mind was a jumble; he hoped he had included a plate in his paraphernalia that was tied up in his bundle. He took his bedroll off to the side a bit, noticing Sid was keeping an eye on him. Jack was sweating bullets as he untied the ragged rope. He unrolled it, and there was a cup and a plate with a spoon, knife, and mismatched fork tied to it. As he rolled the bedroll back up loosely, he whispered a "Thank You" to the lord.

As Jack passed Little Ma going to the food pot, she patted a log beside her and gave him a brief glance. He dipped up a modest amount and then wondered, "Should I go sit with her?" His uncertainty must have shown on his face. He glanced at Sid, who was sitting somewhat close to the old lady. Sid motioned slightly with his head for Jack to go sit by her. He thanked her and took the seat the little lady offered him. He noticed a number of logs in a pile a ways into the bushes. It looked like someone had cut down a rather large tree and cut some of it into stumps. Turned on end, they made good seats. Pretty resourceful, thought Jack as he comfortably, but nervously, sat.

Jack was anxious as he forked a piece of the stew. The voice whispered to him, "Say a prayer of thanks, Jack.

"Oh gosh, thanks Shiny Man." He bowed his head as he held the fork with the food on it and said a hurried prayer softly: "Thank You so much, Lord, for where You have led me. Thanks for having that fellow where he could see me and invite me to join them. Thanks for their accepting and feeding me. I'm so hungry. Amen".

Jack's nerves made it hard for him to swallow what was on his plate. Forcing himself, he cleaned up everything. He even tipped the plate to drink every trace of liquid on it.

Now what? He waited and noted what seemed to be a community dishpan, which everyone was going to. Sid held off until he was about the last one. As he leaned over and took Little Ma's plate, he said sort of loudly with a big grin, "I ain't washing it fer ya, Pard; you got hands."

A few others grinned slightly. Jack followed him over to the dishpan, which was filled with hot, soapy water. The water was too hot to touch. Sid picked up a long-handled pair of pliers, dipped his and the little old lady's plates, one at a time, into the nearly boiling soapy water, and scrubbed them with a long-handled brush that hung by a wire hook on the side of the dishpan. He washed each tin plate and then dried them with a rag that was hanging on another hook. There were so many things Jack wouldn't have thought of. When everyone had washed and dried their dinner wear and makeshift silverware, the rags they dried the eating equipment on, went into the boiling water to sanitize for ten minutes. Then they were pulled out with the pliers and rinsed with clear water and hung out to dry in fresh air—sun, if the sun was still out. Jack was intrigued with their means of survival in safety.

CHAPTER 17

Into The Refiner's Fire

The sun was rising over a faraway hill, making dancing patterns through hanging branches of the trees. Everything was so quiet. Jack greeted the new day with a prayer of thanksgiving. The evening before—was it real or was it a dream? Going over it all in his mind he remembered the stew in the big pot, washing his plate in the boiling water, and then finding a spot where Little Ma had motioned him to go with a flip of her tiny thumb. No one objected, so he moved his bedroll there, and evidently it was then his. As bedrolls were rolled out and with everyone retiring he followed suite. Lying back, he was soon asleep, lulled by the sounds of many snores—some loud, some soft, some sounding like a jumbled chorus.

He wondered if he snored.

When he awoke he saw Sid moving about on his pallet. Jack rose up on one elbow. Sid noticed him awake and stood motioning for Jack to follow. A few yards, away he noticed the trees were closer together than where the group slept. As they walked, he could hear the cars on the highway. Several shovels were leaning against one of the trees. Sid handed him one of the shovels and said, "Choose a tree that's not marked, and be sure you dig deep." Jack understood what was happening, as his bladder was starting to complain. As he moved away to scout out *his* tree, Sid softly called to him, saying, "Dig ya a pretty deep latrine. Put some of the dirt back. Don't forget to bring back the shovel—clean!" Using the shovel, Jack carved "J. H." on the tree over the hole. He was amused at the ingenuity of these guys.

He later noticed Little Ma go away in the opposite direction.

When Jack got back, he saw that his blanket and quilt were spread out and that all of his things had been set out in a neat row. Freezing in place, a casual search found his cell phone safe. He had been systematically searched for the safety of the group. His heart was warmed, and he had to smile. A small wooden box with a lid on a hinge was sitting alongside his stuff. There was lettering on the lid: "BOX STAYS WHEN YOU LEAVE."

He noticed, in particular, that his French harp had been polished and glistened. Nothing was missing, and relieved his cell phone had apparently not been discovered.

Pard's transition had taken place. With a crooked sideways grin, a wink, and a swipe with his hand across his throat, Sid let Jack know that he had been "broke in" and was now on his own.

He put almost everything away in the box but the French harp. He then sat Indian style real close to his loose bedroll just in case anything went wrong, and started softly playing on his French harp, some of his favorite tunes with some church hymns mixed in. He could tell most of the fellows were listening, even though they didn't bother to look at him. Little Ma, however, came and sat *Indian style* beside him. She drew things in the dust with a stick as she listened. Day two was going pretty well.

Out of the shadows came a booming interruption from the big man that Jack had seen the first time he noticed the camp: "Stop that blasted d—— noise!"

As the huge *threaten-er* advanced toward him, Jack rose to try to protect himself. None of the others seemed to be startled—not even Little Ma.

Before the big man reached him, though, a loud two-finger whistle filled the camp—a long shrill and two short ones. Jack stood transfixed. What was going on? Something told him it was critical, perhaps even life-threatening. Sid was on his feet like a self-appointed "in charge" guy.

The big man disappeared. Jack quickly retied his bedroll—with the box.

Once all of them were on their feet, each person began doing a job. They were a well-trained defense troop. There was no doubt that special whistle meant business—like, disappear?

The cook and Mr. Brawn carried the food box to safety in the same direction that Hitch went with the little stove and dishpan.

The warming barrel was doused in the close-by pond. Damp dirt was shoveled onto the hot spot. The shovels were tossed into the bushes.

Somebody else took Hitch's particulars and his bedroll, someone took the cook's, and another took Mr. Brawn's.

All of the others took their own possessions and ran in the same direction.

Little Ma grabbed her bedroll, with all her possessions rolled inside, jumped to her feet, and motioned to Jack to follow her. As she started to run she stumbled and fell, twisting one of her fragile ankles. Jack instinctively scooped her up in his arms, along with both his and her belongings, and struggled to keep up with the others.

With Little Ma in his arms, his bedroll on one shoulder, and Little Ma's bedroll on his other shoulder, he couldn't keep up.

Stopping to catch his breath, Jack held onto Little Ma, leaned against a tree, and closed his eyes for only a moment. Someone snatched Little Ma out of his arms, another roughly tore the two bedrolls from his shoulders, still another, dragged him along by his collar and shoved him into a hard-to-see cave that was hidden by vines that hung down before the entrance.

As they were pressed into the cave, everybody made room for him and no one objected—except for the big man. The big man was unreasonably angry when he saw Jack, the intruder who had become a favorite and been singled out by Little Ma. Jack even seemed to be quietly admired by many of the others. And now he had joined them in their secret hiding place. The big man wanted to kick him out.

Jack was not doing too well. Reality escaped him momentarily. They were crouched and crowded in this damp, smelly cave, hiding from something or someone. All at once, the big man was hovering over him. Jack knew he was going to die right there.

This little lady—this little, old, shriveled-up lady, was holding off the big guy's arm with her tiny, gnarled hand. "He's all right, Bear; leave him to me. He's all right; leave him be."

Wondering about the name she called him, Jack remembered one of the braver fellows saying to the man, "Man you stank, pal; you oughta go jump in that lil ole water hole back there, 'ceptin the water stanks worse 'n you." The big man became "Stank" after that to everyone but Little Ma. He was still Bear to her.

Looking up into those wild eyes as the big man held him down, Jack wondered at his chances of surviving with a recognizable, functional body. He felt he had never been so scared in his short life.

Stank shakily held his temper; he was ready to smash Jack's face, but he hesitated. As he waited, Jack thought that the man's huge fist looked like a persuasive boulder ready to finish him off. He had never been so scared in his life. He was so scared he felt as though he was going to wet his pants.

"Help me, Lord. Please help me," Jack said.

At these words, the big man's temper became fired up to a roaring flame. Jack guessed he must have passed out, because when he opened his eyes, he was slowly gaining consciousness. A hand was over his mouth, and he labored to get air into his lungs. Through half-seeing eyes, he was aware of someone bending over him with a knife at his throat.

"Make a noise and you're done for!" the one bending over him said.

Jack nodded as best he could. The old lady was close by; clinging to someone they called Henry. Jack reached out to her, and she grasped his hand and came to kneel beside him. She was softly crying.

"Did you set us up?" The knife wielder was pressing dangerously hard with the knife. "He wouldn't a picked me up and ran if'n he set us up, Bear. Let 'im go for now, okay?"

"One holler and you're done for," the big man said with a growl as he removed his hand and dropped the knife. He slowly stood up as best he could under the low ceiling of the cave.

Jack could feel the big man still keeping an eye on him. He took note of his surroundings and tried to reason out everything that was going on. A faint candlelight was extinguished, and all movement stopped, except for Jack's thundering heartbeat. He could sense the big man still close by him.

Jack must have fallen asleep, for when he awoke, he could see several people, including the elderly lady, sitting here and there; making no noise. A small opening to the cave was letting in some light. As Jack stirred, the little old lady crept silently toward him with a biscuit in her hand. Just looking at the biscuit made him realize how hungry he was. He felt as if his stomach was trying to wrench its way out of its moorings. He gratefully reached for the biscuit. It was hard and cold. He nodded in thanks to her. As the biscuit went down his dry throat, he found it surprisingly satisfying. Jack began to relax. He could just barely make out a faint smile that played at the corners of Little Ma's small, puckered mouth. Jack then figured he had a friend.

Staying quiet and hidden, Squirrel was again thoroughly enjoying his perch, high in the huge tree, as he watched the frustrated and angry police scurrying around below, trying to find their prize. The policeman in charge had, for a long time, heard reports of homeless people being in that area, and he had taken it upon himself, to bring them in. It became his one goal before he retired, and each failure strengthened his determination. He even had a special squad, and they all enjoyed the hunt. They called themselves "Triple Double Exers"—a rather childish name, but it made doing the work more fun.

The police finally gave up, got back in their cars and left. After hearing the all-clear signal, a long piercing whistle from Squirrel, everyone spilled out of the cave. The big man was calm, mildly, curious, and a bit in awe of Jack as he saw him again pick up Little Ma and carry her back to their space in their world close to the underpass. Somehow their two bedrolls mysteriously showed up a few moments later. No one owned up to bringing them back.

"Good job Fellas. How many times has it been now?"

Things seemed to return to normal for the group. Squirrel came down from the tree to celebrate with them.

Someone gave him a found cigarette butt, and everyone lit up. They felt pretty proud of their added victory; the police had once again been thwarted.

C H A P T E R   1 8

Sharing The Good News

With everyone back at their own interests, Jack took out his small Bible and began to read, to pray, and to give thanks for their victory and for his survival. Little Ma found interest in everything Jack did, so it was no surprise when she limped over and sat beside him. Jack was aware of the warmth in his heart for these people. He was sure of the presence and protection of the Holy Spirit. He also thanked God that the guardian angels had been placed there on duty.

Satisfied and grateful for Little Ma's company and her curiosity, Jack felt that he had become a part of the group. She started putting her finger on the page when he read, meaning, "Tell to me what the marks say." Reading from where she pointed, Jack said, "Come unto me all who are weary (Matt 11:28)—that means tired, Little Ma. Are you tired? She nodded and touched the page again, and Jack continued.

"Tell her, Jack," that small still voice said.

Wondering if she was saved, Jack ventured forth. "Little Ma, do you know God?"

With a question on her face and trust in him, a sweet softness stole across her face. "I think I use'ta. My mama tol' 'bout Him when I was little. She tol' me He had a lil boy too." Little Ma became as a sponge, soaking up the meaning of Jack's words and explanations.

"Little Ma, do you know Jesus?"

One of the men came strolling over to them. "What'er youse talkin' bout? Hey! That's a Bible!" Little Ma smacked his hand as he reached for it, saying to him, "Shorty, you jes git."

Jack's eyes flew open wide, and his eyebrows lifted in unbelief, "Shorty!" he thought. "That man has to be six foot two or three if he is an inch." Jack continued, "He can stay, can't he, Little Ma?"

"Hmph, I guess so."

Still looking at Little Ma, Jack included the six-foot-three fellow, saying, "Shorty, I just asked Little Ma if she knows God." Jack wanted Little Ma to include Shorty by having her share what they had been talking about, so he encouraged her to repeat what she had just shared with him. Still holding her attention, he asked, "What did you tell me about when you were a cute little bitty girl?"

The heavenly glow came back to Little Ma's face. Her eyes held a faraway glistening as she was taken back in time. "My Mama tol' me I had a Pa in heaven and He had a little boy who was my brother named Jesus, an' I guess that's about all."

A lot more facts were going to have to take root in Little Ma's mind, but what she had was really good. He softly said under his breath, "Here is one of the Lord's precious children."

Another thought came to him in his spirit; he more felt the words rather than heard them. "It's simple, Jack. Don't complicate it."

"Your Mama was talking about God, Little Ma. God is your pa—your Father—and He's mine too. Would you like to go see Jesus?"

"Why, shore."

"God and His Son Jesus know more than anyone else. They know everything. They are stronger than anyone else and can do more than anyone else. They can even know what we are saying and what we are doing right now, and that's all right because they love us and help us do good things. They will even come and live inside of our heart if we ask them too. All we have to do is ask them to come in."

This got a wide-eyed look from Little Ma.

"Wal shucks, Jack, let's do it."

"What do you think, Shorty? Do you want to have Jesus live in you?"

"You know, that sounds right good to me."

As he knocked on Pastor Ed's study Jack hoped he had time to talk.

Pastor Ed was happy to see Jack when he opened the door, and ushered him into his office. He turned as he closed the door, and stood for a moment, "Well I don't think I need to ask how things are going with you. I can see by your face!"

Jack's face was radiant. "I'm sure you know the answer."

"I can only halfway guess. Tell me what I hope to hear."

"Well, Pastor Ed, you might be more than half right. Little Ma accepted Jesus as her Savior. God has given us the key person in that group. That's not all. One of the most inquisitive fellows ther came waltzing over as Little Ma and I were talking, and he stayed as I told Little Ma about Jesus. Just out of the blue, Shorty started weeping, fell down on his bony knees, and began apologizing to Jesus for *running out* on Him. Falling almost on his face, he told Jesus how he had missed Him and told Him how sorry he was for leaving, and told Him how sorry he was for all his sinning since running away. He poured out his love to his Father God."

Jack went on excitedly, "Looking up unashamedly, he started telling us how he had been saved in his teens. He told us about how he got so busy running around with girls that he forgot all about God—the God who had made him so full of happiness when he accepted Him into his heart. He said he hadn't felt that happiness since. With repentance and taking hold of the Lord's forgiveness, Shorty knew he was forgiven and brought back into fellowship with his Lord and Savior."

"Little Ma stared open-mouthed at this six-and-a-half-foot man called Shorty, grabbed my arm, and declared, 'Jack, I wants that happiness, I wants to born again—without the running away and sinning. I wants that Jesus to live in me like you said and like Shorty seez he usta have Him.'"

"Pastor, she has just walked around ever since with a heavenly grace about herself. As an added blessing, I noticed Shorty talking to some of the other guys. Myself, I just walk around saying, '"Thank you Lord, thank you Lord."'" Jack had to sit down to compose himself; he was so taken with joy over what the Lord had done.

Shaking his head in wonder, Jack continued. "An even more astounding work of the Lord I witnessed was a miracle for sure. I had noticed this big fellow creeping closer to us out of the shadows; I was not sure what he was going to do.

"That same evening, during supper, with all the guys sitting around together, I sort of hid and watched and listened to Stank—uh, the big fellow—as he finally went and sat among the group while they all ate. He began laying out the whys and wherefores of what they were missing in their lives."

Jack kept pouring out the news about the big man as he slapped his knee. He pumped his fist in the air in celebration and continued. "Stank laid aside his plate—no less a miracle, as much as he loves to eat—and counted off, on his fingers, the good things they were letting pass them by. Someone challenged the big man, saying, 'How do you think you know all this stuff, anyway?'

"Making no excuse about his present condition, the big man

hammered his point into their minds, "Because, I am an ordained minister and walked out on my congregation for they were a bunch of hard-hearted people just like you guys."

Pastor Ed had to think all this over. As he rubbed his chin, a thought occurred to him. "Jack, do you suppose your being willing to open the road of salvation to Little Ma, which brought back Shorty's repentance for sliding away from the Lord—do you suppose that may have helped open the big man's heart so he could reveal his true identity to the group?"

"I hadn't thought of anything like that. Yes, I'm sure it could have."

"It's just a thought that occurred to me, and I feel pretty good about it. Sometimes it takes only one person bold enough to let Christ show in them. Then others can feel safe to do the same. I remember one time my wife, Penny, had to have a shot in the base of one of her fingers because when she would bend it for long, she would have to use her other hand to straighten it. This eventually happened to the same finger on both hands. The doctor said they called it a 'trigger finger.' The doctor's nurse gave Penny a solution and a hand brush. She was told to scrub the whole surface of her arms and hands, up to her elbows, for ten minutes before the shot.

"The shot in the right hand I could—yes, they let me stay with her—I could see it was uncomfortable, but she did well as the medication went slowly in. However, we all were surprised at the entry of the needle into her left finger. Penny involuntarily screamed and then began to yell, "Oh, oh, 'Jesus, Jesus; Father; Holy Father; Oh, Holy Father; Jesus," with tears streaming down her face.

"The nurse had rushed to her side when she started to cry out and put her hand on her shoulder. When the medication was in, the doctor turned to take care of the used needle and other things, saying, "I must have hit a nerve--I didn't want to take it out and start in again, taking the chance of hitting a nerve again."

Penny quickly said, ""That's alright. I apologize. It's over with and didn't last long. I'm sorry."

Pastor Ed went on, "The nurse moved away, saying nothing. My wife was embarrassed at her cries and outburst, and she apologized, again saying, 'I'm sorry. I hope you are both Christians.' There was silence; we were all speechless.

"No one spoke for a few moments. The nurse finally said, "Well, I am."

After a moment or two, the doctor looked at his hands and quietly said, "I am too." We had a great Lord Jesus conversation there in the doctor's office." Pastor Ed's smile was a mile long as he beamed.

"As we were leaving, the doctor and I shook hands, and with a serious face, the doctor said, 'That, lady is going to heal quickly.' On the way home, Penny's fingers began to work like new."

Jack had to get up and pace a bit. He sat down again, putting his hands on his knees as if needing support, and he said, "God works wonders when He has the—ah yes, the opening. " A slow smile crossed his face as he took everything in, thinking about the nurse and doctor for a moment longer. Looking at the floor, he shared more. "Pastor, this huge man, with his big voice, is telling those men what stupid … uh … dopes they were to let themselves be cheated out of the best thing in life."

Shaking his head and rubbing his hands over his face, Jack said, "I could have never gotten by with saying that to those men—the things and the way Stank was telling them about the gift of the Lord's salvation."

Jack relayed the unbelievable tale Stank had told them. "Here's what he was telling them; see what you think of this. I can still feel the force that crept over me as I sat by Little Ma, listening and eating my food.

"Standing tall, Stank shouted, 'You hard-hearted, stubborn blokes, that is why I left my pulpit—I was so disgusted with my congregation for taking advantage of all the gifts God was giving them. Some had yachts, and some were lawyers and doctors, but they just pretended to love the Lord. No! They loved the good life the world was giving them—the good life that they would lose when they went to hell! They didn't care about anyone else that was without. I quit 'em; I was afraid I was gonna hurt 'em in their ignorance. I was through. I walked out; my wife and I just left it all. She wanted me to go back, but I couldn't. I'm a little sorry I didn't go back, because my wife got sick from pining away over my loss of my pulpit. She just gave up and died." Jack had to stop and take a deep breath. "Can you believe all of that?"

Jack continued. "Pastor Ed, I had to quickly move back to where I had been sitting with Little Ma because that big fellow started looking around. I had no idea what he would do if he knew I was listening to what he was telling them. Now, I wasn't eavesdropping—not exactly. We all eat together, or close by, so I couldn't help but hear him."

Still sitting in amazement, Jack shook his head back and forth. "Pastor Ed, he must have been a pastor with a fairly large church, this tattered fellow with wild hair and beard—wilder than mine." Jack added with a smile, "What do you think?"

Pastor Ed and Jack spent a good long time in the sacristy of the church. They just felt the need to give thanks for what had happened back with the group, and to pray for what the Lord would be doing there in the future. They prayed for the big man and for the reason God had him there. Jack wanted especially to pray for Little Ma. Her leg wasn't getting any better. She had seemed a little feverish, and it deeply concerned him. It was hard to tell for sure how bad it was since she wanted no one "fussin" over her. Jack and some of the others there had tried to get her to the hospital, or at least to a doctor. She wouldn't hear of any part of it.

Going to the restroom at the church, Jack cleaned up somewhat so he could go to the store for some supplies for Little Ma. She at least agreed to that much. While he was washing up, an idea came to his mind—Jill—the church. He thought it was far-fetched, but he decided to ask Pastor Ed about it. When Jack got back to the office, Pastor Ed was sitting at his desk with his elbows on the desk and his chin in his hands, almost as if he was quietly praying. Another person had just come in to see him, so he couldn't take Jack to the drugstore, but it was only a few blocks away. They agreed that Jack would return after he made his purchases. He motioned Pastor Ed out the door and said, "I'll need my credit card, Pastor. I sure hope you kept it for me and didn't give it to your wife to go shopping with!"

Snapping his fingers and acting disgusted, Pastor Ed said, "Now why didn't I think of that? I sure dropped the ball there." With a soft punch on Jack's arm and a big smile, he went to his safe and retrieved Jack's card. The look on his face as he handed Jack the card told Jack what was on his mind. Pastor Ed was still in deep thought about the good news Jack had relayed to him.

As Jack headed down the hall, to the outside door, Pastor Ed quietly called to him, "See you in an hour or so. Hurry back, son."

Jack was thankful that he had been able to get a ride into town with some kind farmer whom the Lord had surely sent along at the needed time. He was also thankful for Pastor Ed saying he'd take him back, most of the way, if not all the way. They had so much to talk about. Pastor would have loved to been able to go to their campsite, but how could Jack have explained that clean-looking fellow? It would have taken a lot of explaining and it most likely would have given away his secret of being there undercover. "Patience, patience," thought Jack.

He silently prayed, Thanks for bringing Pastor Ed and myself together, Lord.

CHAPTER 19

Unexpected Meeting

Standing in line, at the drugstore, to check out her purchases at the cash register, Jill was disgusted with the appearance of a man standing in another line who was staring at her with disbelief written on his awful hairy face.

Who is that man … is that … it can't be! Yes, it- I, Oh it is Jack! As her purchases were being rung up, she stared back at him and noticed he was backing out of line. As she stood frozen in her tracks, the next customer in line jolted her back to the moment with the cart. Jill's heart was racing as she paid for her purchases and then stumbled away after the clerk put everything in her cart.

Not about to lose track of Jill again, Jack left his cart and rushed through everyone to her side. Would she talk to him? Would she admit she recognized him, or would she want nothing to do with him? Her face plainly showed him that she was very hurt.

In a panic, she started to leave her cart to get out of the store. Jack grabbed her arm and her cart, and he led her out the door and into the parking lot.

As he stood holding her elbow, a question tumbled out of his mouth: "Where's your husband—or boyfriend? Tell me." Jack couldn't decide if she was going to slap him, curse him, or faint. Gently, with caution, he pulled her to him.

She fell against him and began to quietly weep. "Where have you been? What have you been doing? Where is your wife?"

"I don't have a wife! You're supposed to be my wife, remember?"

Grateful that she was not fighting him, Jack led her toward an isolated area, holding her up and pulling her cart as they went.

A store guard ran up and roughly put his hand on Jack's shoulders. "Hold up, fellow; turn loose of this lady and put your hands in the air." With disbelief, the guard saw Jill's arms go up and around Jack's neck.

Taking a step back, the guard said, in no uncertain words, "Okay, what's going on here? Lady, is he forcing himself on you?"

Jill sighed deeply as she turned her head to the guard. With a weak smile, she struggled to get her voice operable--surprisingly said, "No, he's my fiancée."

The guard's mouth dropped open; he shook his head as he rubbed the back of his neck with one hand. He let out a deep breath and spoke to the crowd that was starting to gather. "Okay, folks, everything is all right here; please go on about your business."

The guard turned back to the couple and looked Jack up and down in disbelief. As he compared how Jack was dressed and how Jill was dressed, his gut told him something was not on the up-and-up.

He said to Jack, "Go back and get your purchases—pay for them, of course—and come back here. We need to have a little talk."

Knowing that he looked dirty and tattered, Jack gave no resistance to the guard's orders. Jack looked behind him as he went back into the store. His face was strained with astonishment, for the guard stayed with Jill, calming her down.

Not knowing just which way to go, he was grateful to the clerk as she called to him. "Come on up, sir, and let's get you checked out." The onlookers, anxious to see the finish of that unusual happening, stepped aside for Jack to go ahead. As she tallied his items, she quietly, in almost a whisper, said to him, "Your lady is in good hands; Fred is a trustworthy guy."

With shaking hands, Jack paid for his things with his credit card, gathered up the bag, thanked everyone with a wave, and hurried out to the car Jill was then sitting in. The guard gestured to him to stand at a distance.

The guard was standing by his car's back door, waiting for Jill to get control of herself. This was frankly an unusual situation, but Jack felt he could trust this professional-looking person. It looked like he was at least more than willing to give it a chance to be worked out.

"Miss, do you want me to arrest this man?" the guard asked. "I will see to it that he gives you no more problems. You don't even have to see him again, and he won't know where you will be. We'll see that you get to your home safely."

With wide eyes, a definite shake of her head, and a sniffle, Jill bolted up straight, dried her eyes, and said to him forcefully, "Oh no, we have just found one another after being separated for over three years."

Words started pouring out of her mouth so fast that the guard could hardly keep track of what she was saying. At first her explanation was one of amazement, but then it changed to concern, and then to anger. The longer she talked, the madder she got, until she was yelling not at him, but just at what was inside of her. She got so mad that she started to cry again.

The guard held his hand up to quiet her. "See if you can compose yourself while I go talk to him," he said.

He walked toward Jack and stopped him from going any farther by putting his hand on Jack's arm. With his eyebrows arched, he said, "I don't know if you want to go talk to her right now; she might black your eye—maybe both of them—before I can stop her. Boy, is she ever sore at you."

"She has every right to be. I have been so stupid and so frantic. I have tried everything I could think of to find her—everything but getting in touch with her parents. I didn't want to scare the socks off of them."

Jack was curious about whatever it was that Jill had actually been yelling at the guard about when he came walking out of the store. She looked madder than he'd ever seen her, even madder than when she broke up with him. He had to stop his heart from racing in his chest or *he* would keel over. That was the first time he had ever seen Jill carry on that way.

Jack tried to explain things to the guard. "Our lives really got screwed up when she broke up with me just before we graduated from college. Life has been crazy ever since—at least for me."

The guard was looking Jack up and down as he talked. "This is a college man? What in tarnation happened to him to get him in this state of dress?" Considering the looks of Jack, the guard was sure he hadn't had a bath or change of clothes since he and Jill had broken up.

Jill tried to get a hold of her emotions as she attempted to comb her hair, and put on some lipstick while telling herself, everything would somehow come out all right—whatever all right meant. As the guard kept talking to Jack, she began to wonder if he *was* going to arrest him. Might serve him right, the jerk. It made her nervous when she saw the guard put his hand near his back pocket, where his handcuffs were. As she opened the car door and stepped out, she thought that maybe she should go to her car, get in and lock the doors; then she and Jack could talk things over.

When Jack saw Jill get out of the car and start looking around, he panicked. "She's leaving! Man, I can't lose her again! He started walking toward her as he called to her: "Jill, wait!"

He started running, and that frightened her. What would he do to her? He looked mad. She started running to get to her car. Luckily her keys were in her hand, and she somehow hit the door opener and saw her lights flash on. Reaching the car before Jack, she jumped in and locked the doors.

The customers from inside the drugstore who had witnessed Jack and Jill finding one another had come outside, and a crowd began to form again. A voice from the crowd shouted, "Boy, I sure wish I had my video camera; this is better than any movie!"

Jack reached Jill's car as he heard the doors lock. With His hands on her window, he pleaded with her. "Jill, I'm sorry; I'm so sorry, Jill.

The crowd was not about to leave. It was instead gathering even more observers. They started taking sides, yelling advice.

Jill was yelling at Jack. "You're sorry? You are always sorry. Why are you always just sorry?" The last word came out as a wail.

"Open up, Jill, and let me hold you. Please, Jill, open the door, sweetheart; I love you."

The door lock popped up. Jack opened the door and slipped in beside her. She was a frozen ball. A moment or two passed and her arms went up and around his neck.

The crowd roared, and applause broke out. Even the guard, as he walked up, applauded and smiled broadly, showing lots of bright teeth as he motioned the crowd away. Everyone went peacefully, all with neat smiles on their faces and in their hearts.

After waiting a reasonable amount of time, the guard knocked on the window of Jill's car and asked her to unlock the back door, he wanted to put her purchases in the back seat for her. "You had better be on your way, kids; you're causing a traffic jam." He was still smiling as he watched them drive down the street. He hoped Jack would be able to clear up whatever his girl was so fiercely angry about.

The knock at his door brought Pastor Ed the best surprise of his day. Jack stood with his arm around the shoulders of a very lovely girl. Pastor Ed motioned them into his office.

Jack and Jill were both ecstatic although Jack was more so than the girl. All Pastor Ed could see was happiness showing on their faces. He was happy for them, especially for Jack, since he had been with him in his suffering at his loss of her.

Introductions gave Pastor Ed more happiness, but didn't have much time to spend with them. Jack handed Pastor Ed his credit card. Pastor Ed walked to his desk, put it into a desk drawer, and locked it away. He listened to the story of how they had met at the drugstore. Seeing the bag Jack held reminded Pastor Ed of where this compassionate man had been.

"What are your plans now, Jack? I see you must have gotten what you needed for Little Ma."

"Little Ma? Who is Little Ma?" Jill was confused.

Jack was at a loss for words, and Pastor Ed filled in for him. "Jack has been involved with a most important vocation for the past few months; I'm very proud of him."

"You have a job?"

Jill was scrutinizing Jack's clothing, as well as his beard and hair! "Where on earth are you working, and who on earth are you working for?"

Jack's heart fell to his feet. His throat froze up—he couldn't speak.

At that moment, Pastor Ed's secretary notified him that the people of the music committee had arrived for their meeting, and he had to excuse himself.

He rose from his chair, walked around to Jack, and touched his arm. "Let me suggest you two go into one of the Sunday school rooms to talk. I'll be a couple hours with this committee. They have several people who have driven in from out of town, so I'll get back with you. Take your time. I'll take you back to the camp." He showed them out another door.

Before the ambience of being together again started to change, they had exchanged cell phone numbers.

Jack remembered the plan he and Pastor Ed had devised while on their fishing trip together. This included Jill somehow working with the lady in Pastor Ed's congregation with the street people along with Jack. It was much too early to mention anything like that to her now, though.

They sat in one of the rooms in the church, but Jill did not sit at all close to Jack. When he reached out to touch her, she became rigid and tense. "Jack, tell me about your work," she said. Her remark was short and unemotional; she held her head a little high and narrowed her eyes a bit as she observed him.

He blurted out the plain, simple facts in a rather rapid-fire discourse, hiding nothing and soft-pedaling not in the least. "God has called me to work with the homeless, and I'm at the present involved with a rather large group—around twenty. At the moment, I am letting a certain lady down, as she has sprained her ankle and it is giving her a lot of pain. We have tried to let us take her to the emergency room or at least to a doctor, but she will have none of it." Jack got up from his chair and began pacing back and forth in the room where they were sitting together.

"I am a minister of the Lord, Jill, and I feel His grace on me as I do his work."

He had to calm himself. Jill was so important to him. He was having a hard time deciding what to do or say next. He whispered a short prayer: "Help, Lord." he knew he had to give Jill the time she needed to process what had happened in his life. He desperately wanted her to understand. He knew he was going to have a hard time with that, looking the way he did.

"Jill," he said, "I am the same person who fell in love with you in kindergarten, and I have loved you all the while we were growing up. I love you now with all my heart, but I have made so many dumb mistakes, starting when we were in college and I listened to a couple of my professors about what they thought was a fantastic job. That job turned out to be worse than what I was going thru during the horror in college, getting ready for it. What I am doing now is where I have belonged all the time. I am where God wants me. But I want this to work out so we can be together. I want so much for us to get married. I love you."

With her head drawn back and her chin down in a defensive pose, Jill listened to this man she thought she knew through and through. No, she didn't know him anymore. As she lowered her eyes, she noticed the bag on the table. Upon opening it, she saw bandages and salve of some kind. There was an ACE bandage and other types of wrappings for an injured ankle, evidently for the woman Jack knew. Thoroughly misunderstanding, Jill wondered if she might be his new interest.

Jill jumped up, grabbed her purse, and took out her car keys. She stood with blazing fire coming out of her eyes. As she raced for the door, she yelled at Jack, saying, "Just go and take your mercy things to your precious lady friend, and don't for one moment even think about me."

Jill reached the door and made her way outside. There were people coming and going on the sidewalk, and she had to weave her way around them. One man tried to grab her to see what her trouble was. She pushed away from him and others that were stopping. She turned, and in a flash, was scrambling into her car. She locked the doors, started the car and roared out into traffic in one move, just barely missing an oncoming car

She heard Jack shout helplessly. "Jill, she is eighty-eight years old, this is no time for you to doubt me, I love and trust you." He fired desperate prayers heaven ward, "Lord we need Your help. I do want to listen to You and follow Your directions."

Jack was able to get her license plate number, and he offered a prayer for her safety. His mind jerked him back to the other responsibility that lay in deep pain at the campsite, needing his attention. His head was in a whirl. Now he would be losing Jill again. Where would she go? Would she have a wreck at the speed she was going?

He had to get the supplies to Little Ma. As he went back into the church to get the bag, he remembered his mother's guidance about Ephesians 5:20 and said, "Thank you, Lord. I don't understand, but You have come through too many times for me to doubt You now.

He slumped in the chair that Jill had been sitting in, put his head on his arms, the table, and began to weep.

Pulling himself together, he knew he had to be patient for he would get to Little Ma quicker if he waited for Pastor Ed to take him close to the campsite. Thumbing his way was fine when he got a quick ride, but not so good when he had to walk most—or even all—of the way.

CHAPTER 20

Big Man Steps Up

Little Ma wasn't doing so well. The pain in her ankle was very intense. Shorty thought back, to his teen years and remembered people praying for different others in their church. In the middle of their meal, Shorty stood up and said excitedly, "Let's pray for Little Ma. That's what people did at my home when I was a lil boy." Not waiting for any answers, he walked over to the suffering lady, turned, and motioned with his hand to those still eating. "Stank, you wanna say the prayer, or should I?" All eyes turned to the big man. With a fork full of food halfway to his mouth, he stopped and thought about that question. One of the other fellas said, "Weeeelll Stank, we gonna pray er not?"

In his big voice, Stank said, "Let's get to it. And don't call me Stank anymore. Didn't you blokes notice I took a bath in the pond and washed my bedding! I'm Big Man, and don't any of you forget it, ya hear?" He roared the last two words.

He walked over to Little Ma and waited. Finally he repeated someone's remark: "Are we going to pray or not?" The others put their plates down and followed him. As he laid his hand on Little Ma's shoulder, the rest did the same. They about pushed her over at first.

"Ease up, men," Big Man said. He told them that he would pray, and all the others should speak out and just say what was on their mind. "You can all pray whatever you're thinking, if you've a mind to. And if you're not thinking anything decent, just keep your trap shut."

There was suddenly a warm place in this big fellow's heart, and with a small, secret smile, he knew what he was going to do. He was going to educate this wonderful bunch of sinners who had taken him in at the lowest point in his life, and he would have to do it in their own language.

As he looked up to the heavens, he addressed the Almighty with arms outstretched: "Lord God who created all we see about us, we want to first thank You for this good earth and for letting us be a part of it. Now one of our members has a real problem with her foot. The pain she is suffering is something terrible. And, Lord, since You made her and all of us, of course, You know every part of that foot that is having the problem. There is this book, the Bible, that is written about You, and in that book You tell us that we should lay our hands on her like You did when You were down here on this earth that you made. And when you laid Your hands on some of Your sick or hurting people, they got well or quit hurting. So we are laying our hands on Little Ma."

He paused and addressed the others as they took note that they were laying their hands on her. "Easy fellows, your about to shove her over." With his hand on Little Ma, he bowed his head. "You said You love us all, so You love Little Ma, and we do too. We want to ask you to make her foot well. And in your Bible it says to ask for things in Your name, so all of us"—he looked up again—"is that right, you guys? Well, is that right?"

An elbow poke in a rib brought a sudden retort, "Yep, we sure do."

Big Man continued the prayer. "We ask in Your name, Jesus, to heal her foot, make it well and take away the pain."

"Bear, it don' hurt no more. Bear—ah, Bear, ya hear me?"

He looked up. "Okay, Little Ma." He again bowed his head. "And somewhere in that Bible it says we are to thank You."

"It is still bigger'n a watermelon, Bear, but it don' hurt no more," said Little Ma.

Yet again, he looked up. "Okay, Little Ma." And yet again, he went back to praying. "So I say thank You." At that point, he looked around at the others. "How about any of you other blokes?"

A chorus of agreement rang out, "yep, thas right, we do, sure thing, thank ya..."

"And Jesus, I, Pard, say thank You also," said Jack, who had walked in during the prayer.

"Hey Pard, when did you get back?" asked Big Man. He then remembered that he was in the middle of a prayer. "Oh, excuse me ... uh, thank you, Jesus. Thank You, Jesus, for taking away her pain in Your name—"

"Uh, Bear," said one of the others, "when do we say amen?"

"Now we all say it. Amen, amen, amen." Bear got lots of pats on the shoulder and arms.

"Good job, Bear," said Little Ma, as she was smiling while sitting up on her log.

"Yep, it sure is still swollen, but you say it don't hurt no more Little Ma? Really?" asked Shorty.

"No, Shorty, it don' hurt no more."

Shorty was very emotional about this sort of thing. He had to wipe a few teardrops off his face. Some sniffles and choked coughs could be heard here and there among the crowd. Jack stuck out his hand to Big Man and praised his action. There were lots of smiles all around. Little Ma was loved by them all, and with her being in pain, it was paining them. Big Man was concerned. "You all know I did the praying but it was the Lord who took away the pain. Don't' forget who is the Healer."

Everyone watched with curiosity as Jack tried hard to concentrate, getting ready to do what he had to do. He pulled out of the bag, all the stuff, he had gotten at the drug store. Everyone had to crowd around to look everything over. Jack reported that he had gotten a book that explained how to put the bandages on. He was careful to wrap the ankle snugly but not too tightly. Little Ma said, "I jes don' believe how much better it feels. Ah believe the swellin'll be gone in a coupla days."

"Oh, the faith of God's people," Jack quietly said. He again gave his thanks to the gracious, merciful and Holy God.

Little Ma was a good patient and kept off the ankle until the swelling was gone.

Shorty was just happy that the Lord heard their prayers. "You know, Stank—I mean Big Man—I wonder if we cud have some church sometime? Pard, ya cud play the music fer us, ya think?"

CHAPTER 21

A Huge Misunderstanding

Jill knew love was a strong anchor. She felt completely out of control. She softened the pressure on the gas pedal of her car and slowed down to the speed limit. Trying hard not to cry as thoughts whirled in her head, Jack's voice came back to her: "Jill, she is eighty-eight years old!" Had she heard him correctly? Is that really what he said? How is he involved with an eighty-eight-year-old-lady? His grandparents were dead, she knew. What other eighty-eight year old lady did Jack know? Just what was Jack involved in, she wondered. Had he gotten himself into something he couldn't get out of? What happened to the newspaper job he said he had when he came to her college and was trying to tell her he was taking classes for it at his college?

Yes, her mind and thoughts were just crazy. Recognizing the landscape and buildings, she realized she was more than halfway back to where she was living and working. How had she driven seventy-five miles without even realizing the route she was taking? Bile rose up in her throat—fear crept into her heart. Should she turn back or go on? She knew she couldn't face her mother in the state she was in. She pulled into an eatery, parked, and called her mother.

Oh, how she wished she still had her father—that he had not had the fatal heart attack.

The phone rang and rang, but there was no answer. Where could her mother and grandmother be—shopping, perhaps? Well, at least she would not have to answer a lot of embarrassing questions. The call went to the answering service. "Hello, Mom, a mild emergency has come up at work and I have to get back immediately." Well, that was a halfway truth. She knew her mother would worry about the things she had brought with her. "Would you just put my things in the closet—even the luggage. I have more and will pick up those things when I come the next time. So, thanks, Mom. It was so nice seeing you and Grandma, even though it was for such a short time. I had better be getting there, so bye, Mom, I love you. Tell Grandma I love her too."

When she arrived at her apartment, Jill wondered if she had been too hasty in judging Jack about what he was doing. His family and hers had always been church people when they were growing up, but living, as a homeless person was something else. What could he be thinking of, and what did he hope to accomplish? The pastor didn't seem to be off the screen with that sort of thing. The people she saw at the church didn't seem to be homeless people.

She was sure she hadn't gotten the whole picture. Admitting there was a deep anger in her and distrust she still felt toward Jack, she was dealing with her heartache for him. In spite of herself, she invariably compared every guy she met to Jack.

Taking a shower and getting into comfortable pajamas before getting something to eat gave her time to think about what she wanted to do. She wanted to call Jack and apologize, of course. He had to understand the strain she was under when coming across him looking as he did.

After eating and putting her dinner items away, rinsing her dishes, and putting them into the dishwasher, she dug in her purse for the scrap of paper with Jack's cell phone number. "Oh, dear, why do I put so much in my purse?" she wailed as she scolded herself.

"A normal person would think I have my whole office in my purse." she was mumbling out loud as she shook her head with disgust at herself, " My apartment is not like my purse; nor is my desk in my office at work—and here I am babbling to myself like a crazy person. Jack, you've got me crazy. I wish I had you here to talk to."

Jill was getting close to tears again, she took out a few things, and then some more, but she couldn't find the piece of paper she had written Jack's cell phone number on. She took out more and more, and finally dumped everything on her bed as she began to panic. Had she not put the paper in her purse?

She looked in her pockets in the closet and clothes hamper, but the paper was not to be found. Tears of frustration spilled from her eyes. Had she lost it? That couldn't be. Anger began to rise in her.

The car! She hoped it was there. Grabbing her keys she ran to the garage as the tears started again. "Lord, let it be in the car; let it be there, please." It wasn't on the seat, and it wasn't on the dash. She ran her hand along the side of the seat—no paper. Had she left it at the church? She would call tomorrow to see if someone had found it or if someone would give her Jack's number. In disappointment, she laid her arms on the steering wheel, thrust her face into her arms and bellowed—Oh, and there it was! She spied the crumpled piece of paper on the floor, through the space between her arm and the wheel. Now she remembered. She was so angry and frustrated that she had simply crumpled up the paper and thrown it onto the floor. "Thank You, Lord. I'm sorry I got mad again; please help me control my temper."

Overjoyed, she reached for the paper, saying a thousand more thank-you's. She then bounded back into her living room. She knew she would not make sense right then; she needed to calm down before calling Jack.

She tried to form an intelligent reason in her mind to tell Jack why she had fled so insensibly. Her mind shook her. "Just be honest, dear, tell it as it is." The thought came to her that possibly Jack had been in similar straits about writing to her and dealing with all the work of his many different classes while they were in college. Had she been unreasonable in her expectations of him toward writing to her? Of course not! All he had to do was scratch a few lines to her and drop it in the mail, as she did everyday for him while they were in college.

How tired she was. She knew she had tried to cram too much into today. Her eyes would not stay open. Just a few moments more and she would tackle those two phone calls. Yes, it would be easier than getting paper, pen, envelope, and stamp and then having to take them to the closest post office. A relaxed moment was all she needed. Just a few minutes more and she would call; she was so tired.

Jill's mother and grandmother were concerned about the message Jill left on their answering service; it was necessary for her to return to where she was living and working. What could the emergency possibly be?

Grandma was the first one to put her concern into words, "Janet, I feel concerned that Jill hasn't called to let us know she made it back to her apartment all right. Do you suppose we should give her a call?" Jill's grandmother had been staying close to the phone. She worried about Jill driving on those dangerous highways. "We know Jill is a good driver, but you can't always depend on some other drivers."

"Very true, Mother. Let's give her until before we go to bed; then we'll call her if we haven't heard from her. She probably has a lot to do since she has to go to work tomorrow. Let's give her a little more time. By the way, did you find the bag of yarn you wanted to use for the scarf you thought of making for Jill? I think she will appreciate it because she is farther north now and it might be somewhat colder in the winter."

"No, I haven't. I was sure I put it in my knitting bag, but it's not there. I'll have to look in the dresser drawers in the sewing room. I really would like to start on it."

"Want me to help you look in there?" Janet started walking towards the sewing rom. "That would be a reasonable place to put it. I remember you brought it home, so I know we didn't leave it. You showed it to me as you compared the dye number with the yarn you had left over from the sweater you made, so it is all together— somewhere!" They had to smile at one another because of their occasional forgetfulness.

As they looked for the yarn, which they found in one of the drawers in the sewing room, they got distracted and found many other interesting things there to look at. As they found various things in the drawers, they had a lovely time remembering how they each had given sewing lessons to their young daughters.

Glancing at her watch, Jill's mom declared, "Oh dear, it is eleven o'clock. We had better not try to call Jill this late. She is most likely fast asleep. We can call her first thing in the morning. Even if we don't get her before she leaves for work, we can still call her later on her cell phone. Thank the Good Lord for cell phones. Whatever did we do without them when we were younger?" That got an amused little giggle from Jill's grandmother.

"Yes, you're right; I'm too tired to make any good sense talking at this hour, anyway."

The two ladies agreeably went to their separate rooms to go to bed, each one still a bit ill at ease but not wanting to worry the other. It would be all right. They would call in the morning.

Jill had insisted to them that it was no problem at all for them to call anytime they felt they needed to talk to her, even at work. She didn't worry about either of them calling her at work, because they were both so nervous calling her then that neither of them would talk long at all.

The next morning Jill opened her eyes to find she had fallen asleep on the couch last night and that it was daylight—late morning. Jumping up, last night's shower would have to do. Grabbing the first suit and blouse her hands lit on would do. Her numerous shoes usually worked with most everything she had. Ready and out the door, into the car she was on the way to work. She parked her car, ran into her office building, and pushed the button on the elevator. After rushing past fellow workers with a hurried good-morning, she got to her office to find her desk piled with pressing work. Her good friend Jan stuck her head in the door. "Hey, the boss has been buzzing for you, my friend!"

With a quick knock at his open door, she received his hearty, but surprised, answer: "Jill, come in."

"Mr. Tyler," she said, "I am so sorry I just got here. I have had a very trying two days and overslept this morning. I do apologize." She was thinking in her heart, "I also have some apologizing to do to Jack, Mom, and Grandma!"

"It's quite all right," he said. "'To whom much is given, much is required'—or something like that. I don't remember where I read that, but it sounds like it could fit with your two days, somehow or other."

He was a little amused at the flustered state of this usually efficient and dependable young lady who helped make his responsibilities much lighter. The day went well and Jill finished everything she had to do.

That day back to work after the long weekend was exceptionally busy, and Jill was worn out as she drove home. The highway was bumper-to-bumper. Resolving not to let the drive home add to her tension she turned on some soft music and let it soothe her. The first thing she wanted to do after she got home, opened her door, and took off her shoes was too call her mother and grandmother.

"Hello, Mom, this is your rapscallion daughter. Will you—can you—forgive me for not calling you sooner?" She took the time to patiently tell her mom all the gory details of what had happened the night before. She didn't try for sympathy, though she was willing to accept it if that was what her mom felt like giving her. She simply stated the facts.

"Is Grandma awake? Would you turn on the speaker phone?"

As they talked together, the tension drained away for all three of them. Jill apologized again for not calling sooner, and she satisfied any questions asked by her mother and grandmother. "I would like to ask you both to pray for me," she said. "I saw Jack at the drugstore, and yes, I still love Jack and want no one else. I'm going to call him and see what Jack is thinking. I was pretty rude to him and realize now that I was probably expecting too much from him while we were in college. He had more courses to deal with than I did. I will let you know how we come out"

"Well, you and Jack have been very close—almost inseparable—since kindergarten, so go for it if that's what your heart tells you."

"Thanks, Mom, I appreciate that."

"But don't let him pull any wool over your eyes, though. Don't let him tell you a bunch of lies, Darling."

"I won't, Grandma. He is just as anxious to talk things out as I am. I'll call you in a few days. Don't hesitate to call me, either of you, if you take a notion to. I'm always so glad to hear from you. I'll say good-bye now and get something to eat."

Their good-byes took some time, as each of them added little instructions on this and that. Jill felt blessed to have such great ladies to care for her and look out for her. She sensibly knew that food was the next thing she needed.

"Be sure you eat healthy, Dear." was one of the instructions.

CHAPTER 2 2

Questions and More Questions

Pastor Ed had dropped Jack off near the homeless camp. When he got there he was greatly relieved and thankful about how God had set Little Ma free of the pain in her foot. He was thankful he wasn't hearing her moan in her sleep at night, as she had been doing before the prayers. He was glad, too, that Little Ma had let him put the binding on her foot. That would support her ankle and protect her from doing further damage to it until it completely healed and strengthened again.

That having been taken care of, he lay awake thinking about Jill. He was heartily giving thanks to God for His help in their finding one another. Now, after she had gotten work after graduation and taken a job where he couldn't find her, God had indeed brought them back together at the drugstore. Jack was convinced that it was no coincidence—it was indeed a God-incident—it was a 'God-wink', as he had read somewhere.

But she had disappeared again. At least they had one another's cell phone numbers. He thought he would call her, but decided to wait for a time to see what God was going to do next. He just seemed to hear, *"Give her space again."* That he would do. He felt a real peace about it.

As he lay pondering all these problems regarding their caring for one another, the idea that had popped into his mind earlier, while he was cleaning up in the pastor's washroom, came to him again. Did it even make sense? Would it put her in danger? He would have to talk to Pastor Ed about it. Yes, it might work—Jill and the street ministry group. Then she would understand. He could tell though, that Pastor Ben still had questions. He would just have to wait it out. God had given him a peace about that.

Jack's improved appearance was noticeable to Big Man. He, too, must have had a bath, but where? He still didn't completely trust this newcomer. He wondered how and where Jack had gotten the money to buy the supplies for Little Ma. Something was going on, and he didn't know if he could trust it. He decided to have a talk with Pard. He also thought it might be wise to take a couple of the other members into his confidence. He had some questions he wanted answered.

Yes, those questions were the place to start. He and Little Ma had always had a fairly close relationship. Why, though, had she immediately teamed up with that newcomer? His reading the Bible most every free moment gave Big Man something to wonder about as well. His getting Little Ma and Shorty saved angered him at first, but then it made him curious, and maybe even a bit jealous.

Almost aloud he muttered, "Is this fellow perhaps a man of God?"

Big Man sat down on one of the stumps near Shorty, pulled out his pocketknife, and began whittling on his most recent creation— an intricate cross. "Shorty, I was mighty glad to hear you rededicated your life to Christ; probably wouldn't hurt for all of us to do that occasionally. When you talked to a few of the others, did you have any success?"

"Well, I don't reckon I know what you mean by success. I wasn't trying to get anything when I tol' them how I came back to God. Or do you m-mean success like when you go out squirrel hunting and don't bring any squirrels back witcha? I don't rightly remember who 'twas that asked me how I felt after I rededicated to Jesus, but I jes told him how happy and free it made me f-f-feel." The poor guy began to stutter as he looked at the knife Big Man held. "Whoever was t-there and listened, it was o-okay with me. If'n whoever was there didn't wanna pay attention, that was okay too. What'd you mean s-success? Like are we gonna have some c-church sometime? How do you feel about doin' that?"

Well, that didn't get him anywhere, but he answered—somehow so as not to upset Shorty any more or set him against him. Shorty had asked that simple Church question twice. "We'll have to consider doing that."

Big Man next looked over at Sid, who was cutting some more corn up for a stew. "Looks like Sid could use some help," he mumbled.

Most of the others were out finding a vegetable garden that would supply veggies for the stew, so it was a good time to talk to him. Big Man hefted himself up to his feet and went over to offer help. With his big hands, he could shuck those ears in no time and break them into pieces or use his knife to make even smaller pieces. "You know, Sid, that was something, you finding Pard by the side of the road. Like finding a puppy or something," he said with a friendly smile. Sid gave a nervous lazy grin. "Yeah, he was a sorry sight. He was as pitiful as a scrounge pup."

"Are you okay with how he has fit in?"

"Yeah, he ain't caused no trouble and has been good company fer Little Ma. Why do you ask? I was kinda sorry 'cause he seemed to trouble you at first. Whatcha thinking? You got somethin' on him?" Sid's eyes were wide open; he was ready for any scuttlebutt.

"No, but I was curious where he got the money to buy the stuff for Little Ma's ankle. That set him back a good many dollars."

"Let's ask him," said Sid. "Pard," he called, "got a couple minutes?"

Jack was happy to do anything; he ambled over. "Sure, want some help?"

"Uh-oh," breathed Big Man, hoping he hadn't opened a can of worms. He motioned for Jack to sit.

"Just happened to have a question come to me," said Big Man. "I might want to capitalize on it if I could. Where'd you get all the cash to buy those things for Little Ma's ankle? Could we go get some too?"

Jack was on to Big Man, but it didn't bother him. "You bet. There's a church I have done some work for, and I get a few dollars now and then. I did some cleaning, and I got the money. Come with me the next time if you need some cash. It's a tough trip into town, but if you're lucky a truck driver will often give a loner a ride. I like to go occasionally. The pastor is a pretty good sort. He's okay with me cleaning myself up a bit while I'm there too. He is not pushy, though. I wouldn't go if he were."

The fellows who had gone in search to find some vegetables brought back a goodly amount, and it all went into the stew pot, along with a rabbit they had trapped earlier. Cook had the rabbit simmering ahead of time.

Jack hadn't lied to Big Man, because one time when Jack went to Pastor Ed's church he visited the popcorn machine and scooped up a good-sized bag. He turned to close the door and dropped the bag. As he tried to catch it, he hit the bag, spreading popcorn over the floor, so that gave him a cleanup job. Neither did he intend to divulge how Pastor Ed did Jack the favor of keeping his credit card in his safe nor how Jack retrieved the card from Pastor Ed when he needed it to pay for the supplies for Little Ma.

Jack was trying to avoid telling any lies. It was too easy to get caught up in lies, which would create the need for more lies to cover up the lies told before. No, he would not go to lies, which could eventually expose his cover, plus he would lose all credibility he may have gained with the group. If that happened, he might not be able to minister the Gospel to them. Little Ma had accepted Jesus as her Savior, and Jack prayed each and every day that the rest of them would do the same. He wanted to be able to walk the streets of heaven with all of them.

Jack had a feeling that Big Man still did not completely trust him. He was just going to have to trust God to give him some of those tools Pastor Ed had mentioned. He reasoned that it had to be real what he told them—and there was Big Man who had been a pastor of a church, and had gotten angered with his congregants "playing church," and how they evidently only gave voices to being Christians in following Christ--so much to think about.

It must have been that Big Man's congregation had observed their faith only in words--not in their hearts; Jack felt that Christ was still in the big man. He had evidently gotten so discouraged by disillusionment that he had just given up.

Jack prayed in his heart, "Lord, don't let that happen to me. Help me to always stay close to you in obedience, trust, faith and love as I serve You."

By getting acquainted with Pastor Ed as he had, Jack learned that pastors needed a lot of prayer as they carried on their work for the Lord. Jack was waiting for the next step, for he was sure Big Man was not completely satisfied. He sure hoped Big Man was not going to explode again. If he did, what would be the outcome the next time?

Big Man's mind was in such a quandary; he indeed worried and knew it would be better to clear the air than to let unanswered questions build into mountains of problems. Straight talk was much better; it was much safer for relationships. Questions raced through his mind: Why was Jack gone for such long amounts of time? Where was he all that time? What had he been doing? Did it spell trouble for their Association, as Sid introduced him to them? Who is he really?

Little Ma satisfied Big Man's curiosity about her fairly close relationship with Pard. Remember, I am a 'filter finder' and I filter out lots of things—Jack's alright."

His reading the Bible most every free minute, however, still gave Big Man something to wonder about.

Big Man had his uneasiness about Pard, but many of the members were noticing a change in Big Man. They wondered if it was a good change? He was a big fellow and could cause *big* trouble if he got out of hand. Did they love or respect Big Man, or were they just afraid of him and trying to keep out of his way? It would make sense why they'd feel that way, especially after seeing his attack on Pard in the hideout cave. It was strange and bothersome to them, also that Big Man used to be a preacher. Most of them were just biding their time to see how this new idea would affect them.

Not wanting to raise any ruckus among their usually peaceful members, they talked quietly among themselves as they observed Big Man and what was in his craw.

"I don't want any trouble here," said Shorty.

"Do ya think the Jesus thing is stirrin up trouble," wondered Sid.

"Yeah! Do they think they're better'n us," added Zeke.

"Ah'm gonna talk quiet-like with you, Shorty, ya allus been easy ta git along with, and you do seem a lot happier," offered Sid. Shorty accepted that observance and nodded his agreement.

Talking among themselves, about a new feeling in their midst, drew them still closer together. They had no gloomy feeling about Shorty's interest in having church. If that would make him feel better, they'd sit in.

They noticed Big Man sitting with Little Ma one day. That didn't bother them. They knew Big Man was always supportive and respectful to her as he would have been to his mother. She could always do a lot to calm him if he got too riled about anything--which he did at times. Everyone else would just move out of his way. They knew He'd rant a bit and then go to his private space and forget everyone. What else could they want? When he quieted down with Little Ma talking to him, he became fairly warm and sociable again.

Big Man got up from talking to Little Ma and disappeared into his private space. Curiosity took hold of the group as they continued their discussion about the business of the association.

"What do ya suppose he has in all his stuff?" Sid craned his neck as he watched Big Man.

Beats me, but I'm not one to invite trouble on myself tryin' to find out." Shorty wanted nothing to do with Sid's question.

"Yeah, why is he so private about what he has?" Zeke was puzzled.

"I don't think he's holding out anything on us, do ya?" suggested Sid cautiously.

"Well he most al'ays seems to feel better after he ducks into his place for a bit." Shorty wanted it settled and forgotten.

"You guys wanna find out? I'll take a look when he gets his shovel and disappears," smiled Sid.

"If'n you do that, you're on your own fer as I'm concerned," proffered Zeke.

"Well no one's askin' ya to be concerned. Ya wanna punch in the mouth?" Sid countered as his short temper began to rile.

"Yeah, if you think yer—"Zeke said as he doubled up his fists.

"Hey, hey, hey! Wait a minute. Look what's happenin' here. We do our own thing, right? If you want to do it, that's up to you, and anybody not wan'in to, it's up to them. We do our own thing, right—an' no gettin' riled like Big Man," said Shorty, as he began to get nervous.

"Yeah, you're right. Sorry, man," offered Sid to them all.

"Yeah, me too, but I ain't sayin' I will or won't do it." grumbled Zeke.

"Yeah, we'll let it go at that," said Sid, keeping the peace. "Course, if ya find out anything interesting, we'd be all ears to hear what ya come up with." Sid's big grin and easy take-it-or-leave-it ways sat fine with the fellas.

CHAPTER 23

The Unveiling

The sun was just barely up, and Jack sat reading his Bible. Sid was moving about. He seemed always to be an early riser regardless of circumstances. He disappeared with his shovel, and on the way back he noticed Jack sitting up with his book again. He wondered what he got out of reading like that. Calling softly to him, he said, "Hiya, Pard."

"Name's J. H."

"Oh, yeah, J. H. Okay. Well, watcha readin' Pard?"

A small smile teased Jack's face as he thought, "Should I get mad?" Another smile spread across his lips, this one broader. "Morning, Sid. Well, my friend, I'm reading the boss's manual. There's a lot in here to think about and follow. I find it really helpful. In fact, I try to do the things He says to do."

Sid ambled toward Jack, and Jack met him halfway so their talking wouldn't wake anyone else, especially Little Ma. She was making up some of the sleep that her pain had recently stolen from her. He held the book out to Sid. "Do you have a Bible?"

"Naw, heard of it though." He took it in his hands and flipped through some pages. "No pit'chures—how come?"

"Well, the pictures come to you—in your mind, in your heart, that is—when you read the words. Can you read, Sid?"

"Oh, I never was real good, but yeah, I can read."

"Sid, do you know what sin is?"

"Sure, ever'body knows about them bad things."

"Here, read this for me." Jack held the Bible out and pointed to a sentence. Sid leaned in close and draped an arm over Jack's shoulder.

Jack felt a shadow of a smile. He saw Sid as a big, lovable kid. "Read it out loud, okay?"

Concentrating on each word, Sid slowly read. "'For all … have … sinned'—Ho, there's that word, Pard—'and come … s-s-short?' What does that mean, Pard?"

"Well, that's like if you're a little kid and you are supposed to do something like pick up your toys, so you pick up all but leave one on the floor 'cause you're too busy or too lazy to pick up the last one—you came short of doing what your mom told you to do. Jack hoped that was clear to the happy-go-lucky guy.

"Well I ain't never had no toys but--Sid's face was full of concentration. He held out one finger and tilted his ear to the right, "You hear that?" He was curious if Big Man was asleep. He thought he heard the big guy talking to himself again. He wondered why he did that. He thought it might be a good idea if he listened—not eavesdrop, of course, but just listen. "Let's go see if Big Man is awake and talking to himself."

Jack laid his "Bible down on a stump, took his shovel and disappeared. He wanted no part of listening in on Big Man's business.

Sid crept quietly over close to Big Man's cleverly built construction. It sounded as though someone was crying big, deep sobs. Is Big Man cryin? He wondered. He went around to the back, where no one would see him. Yes, there was someone crying.

Between sobs and moans, the crying person was speaking. "Lord, I don't mean to question You, but I just have to or go crazy. Forgive me this time; I just don't understand. You called me into the ministry and then, gave me a bunch that claimed to be all serious and holy Christians, but they were just the have-fun-and-get-lots-of-money-to-hang-onto-as-others--kind of so-called Christians. They seemed to be in a contest to see who had the best car and who had the best house.

"The board would okay adding to our church building. They wanted to have the most beautiful church so it would attract more people to join. Our goodwill offering was so pitiful, Lord. I was ashamed to send it in. If I'd mention helping the poor—you wouldn't believe the reasons they would give, talking among themselves about all the expenses they had coming up and why they couldn't help their neighbor. I'd get so mad whenever I'd think about what they thought Christianity was all about. I could hardly hold on to myself in the board meetings. I wanted to get up and knock some Godly sense into them.

"Now, even after I ran away—I'm sorry about running away Lord, but I just could hardly hold on to myself—and now here I am, away from it all, and some of these people I'm with now want church. What do I do now with what they are? Oh, uh … yes. Yes, Lord, yes. But I—oh, okay, Lord. Thank You, Lord. Thank You." Sob, sob. "Yes, I will. Bless You. Yes, thank you. Bless the Lord. Oh, my soul, let all that is within me bless Your Holy Name." Sob, sob. "Sorry about my weeping." Sniffle. "Yes, thank You, amen. Amen, amen. Forgive me, Lord, for whining. Thank You, Lord. Yes, You are my Shepherd. I give You thanks for all things. You do not error, and Your plans for me are so much better than plans I could make for myself. I love You, Lord, and I lift my voice to worship You. You're my King and Savior. Amen."

When he heard the last "amen," Sid crept silently away, his mind spinning. Listening to this huge and powerful man crying and talking to God left him skittish.

"Sid, are you all right?" asked Jack as he came back to where Sid was standing. "You look like you might have seen a ghost. Sid, you okay?"

Because of his own bewilderment, Sid could hardly respond to Jack's questioning face and big eyes. What could he say? Never in all the days of knowing Big Man would he have believed it if someone else had told him he would ever hear Big Man cry or talk to God. He grabbed Jack's arm forcefully. "Big Man's, bawling, like a big kid. An' he's talkin' ta God! Will God kill us all?"

Jack told Sid. "No, I didn't believe God would kill us just because Big Man talked to him with tears," but added that, "If Big Man, got riled enough, he might come out fighting." What could they expect next? Could Little Ma calm him if God hadn't? Where had she taken off-to? "Little Ma, where are you?" called Jack.

To give Sid something to do to distract him from his discovery about Big Man, Jack suggested he go find Little Ma. "See if you can find her and talk her into coming back to her chair—uh—log." he said. "Remind her that she promised to stay off her foot until the swelling is gone."

Sitting in her "private" bush, Little Ma wasn't going to order Sid around, but she had to keep her eye on him because he was a bit quirky at times. Bear could take care of himself, but she didn't want eavesdropping to get anyone there in trouble.

At that moment, Big Man came out of his private place. "Pard," he said, "I want to talk to you."

The command from Big Man brought Jack's attention front and center. "Sure, Big Man, what's on your mind?" he asked.

"This is probably going to come out wrong, but bear with me, okay? I'm going to be out in the open and *blunt*." Big Man was now very serious.

"I have found that that is the best way, but you know what?"

"Okay, let me have it." Big Man wanted to know.

With a chuckle, a grin, and a wave of his hand, Jack hurriedly said, "No, no. I'm glad you gave me some warning. That way I now feel prepared to listen. We can be honest, and blunt, with one another." Jack felt relieved but smiled broadly.

"Yeah, right. All right, here it goes. Ready?"

"Ready." Jack held up his hand for a high five. Big Man relaxed and grinned and slapped Jack's hand.

Big Man became sober. "In a short version, one: when you went for supplies for Little Ma, why were you gone so long? Okay, two: where were you all that time? Three: what were you doing all that time? Now, here's the big question. Four: Does it spell trouble for us in this group, which Sid calls the association? Finally, five: Who are you really? You're too smart to be homeless. Those questions are probably none of our business, yet they could all affect this group of people—this community."

Jack shifted in his makeshift chair and drew his face into a thin grin with raised eyebrows. "Well, I disagree with your last statement--uh—halfway. They are my business, yes, but you have a right to know because you have accepted me, a stranger, into your midst, and if I had a wrong agenda, it could have a harmful effect on this really great, community."

Most of the fellows by then, had gathered around Big Man and Jack, being interested in the questions and the answers.

Jack had to think before making any careless statements that would put him "in a box," so to speak.

"How do you want my answers—hedging a little bit, or just plain, outright blunt answers? I'd rather just be plain honest." He smiled broadly, looking around at each of them.

"I believe we would all rather just have the plain, honest answers, right fellows—and Little Ma?"

"Right, sure, tha's fine; give it to us straight. What's goin on here Bear? Why pound him with all these questions? Wha's he done?" Little Ma questioned what was going on.

Always willing to hear any scuttlebutt, Sid sidled over to Big Man to secretly ask, "What's he done Stank—uh, Big Man?"

Big Man chose to ignore Sid's impertinent remark, and with an unlikely move, Big Man put his hand softly on Jack's shoulder. Jack felt love in that gesture. Everyone looked on, relaxed, yet curious. A general attitude of comradeship settled in. They were ready to listen without already condemning him for whatever it was he might have done.

Big Man gently and sincerely, said to Jack, "Just open your heart to us, Pard."

"Okay, here it is, straight up." Jack began his tale. "My name is Jack Hampstan.

Question number one, two and three: Why was I gone so long? I found my girl while getting supplies for Little Ma at the drugstore, and I took her to meet my pastor at his church—three years earlier she threw me over, more about that later—you will get to meet her. Question number four: No. All this doesn't spell trouble for us here in this group. I even hope Jill, my girl—my fiancée—will somehow, someway become a part us.

"Shall I go on?"

Big Man liked what he was hearing but wanted the whole story. They all wanted more. This was getting to be too good. Sid brought him a hot cup of coffee and gave him a soft touch on the shoulder.

"Thanks, Sid. You guys are hard taskmasters, and this is where it gets tough—for me, that is."

"After graduating from College, I worked for a newspaper and hated it, so quit."

This was making Jack nervous. Would they kick him out? Remembering everything, Jack paused to run his hands through his hair, and he did a bit of stretching and deep breathing. Jack leaped out of his seat at this point; he began to pace and relive the whole experience. He sat down again and looked at the ground.

"In a nut shell, here it is: My girl dumped me, and the new job turned out to be unbearable, I quit, I drove by here one day and saw you all, went back to town, met a great pastor—one like you have here with you." Jack smiled at Big Man. "I got a job at his church, I was born again and filled with the Holy Spirit, then the Lord showed me I was to be here with all of you. That is my story. I'm just a guy who wants to be in God's will, right where He wants me." Jack sat down and dropped his hands onto his knees. He slowly shook his head, "It is almost unbelievable how God has worked all of his out. Big Man, I'm under your direction here. Do I stay or do I go?"

Big Man just sat and stared at Jack for a time. No one said anything.

"Jack, we need to talk," he was finally able to speak.

"Okay, sir. I feel God has made you the boss here."

CHAPTER 24

Understanding Helps Forgiveness.

Jill was getting discouraged, and she was trying to hold on to her temper. She had learned of the bad consequences her temper had lead to; it had almost ruined her life. "Why doesn't Jack answer his phone?" This was the fifth time she had called him with no answer. She wondered if he could see it was her calling and didn't want to talk to her. *No!* That was one of the negative ideas that had helped to separate them.

"I guess I'll just have to pray. Whoa, sorry, Lord. You noticed that bad thought, didn't You? Forgive me; You are the point where I should have started years ago." Her heart was telling her to move back home if she really wanted to get back with Jack. Now she was going to have to have a heart-to-heart talk with her boss.

Because she was so efficient, it was no problem for her to clear up all issues that were her responsibility, so she arranged all the papers her boss needed to sign or approve, and she asked him if he would give her a few minutes before he went home after work.

With her head down, close to tears, apologizing to her boss for letting him down after being so good to her, Jill tried her best to make sense of why she felt the Lord was telling her to go back home.

She was blubbering and talking so fast that Mr. Tyler could hardly get a word in edgewise. He put a firm hand on Jill's arm, and she finally looked up and froze, speechless.

"Jill, I believe the Lord really is truly directing you to go home. You won't believe the phone call I got this morning." He had to check and see if she was all right. "You're not going to faint, are you? I got a call this morning from the young lady whose place you took—the one who used to be my secretary. She wanted to know if there was somewhere we could use her again, as she needs more money. So, you see, most everything works out for the best. If you like, I will do what I can to help you get a job in your hometown—but only if you like. I have been exceptionally pleased, Jill, with your helping me out and coming to working here"

Jill was able to let go and release tears of relief and thanksgiving. Mr. Tyler let her get hold of her emotions before working out her request. He was going to miss her skill in making his days easier, but the young lady coming back was skilled at it also. There would be no breaking in a new secretary. Jill felt much better about that news.

When Jill arrived at her apartment after quitting her job, she excitedly called her mother. "Mom, I'm coming home! I mean I'm moving home. I miss you and Grandma so much. Mr. Tyler understands and has offered to help me get a job there. No more traveling back and forth; I can hardly wait!"

"Oh, sweetheart, I can hardly believe what you are saying, and we do miss you too. Is there anything we can do to help?"

"I can't think of a thing except just receive me when I come back. I will give to Goodwill what furniture I will not need or want. Everything else will fit in my van. I will call you again late tomorrow to tell you when to expect me. I just love you and want to be with you again. Now I feel like a baby, but I just want to be there—at home. My apartment here is just not home to me. I'll call you tomorrow;

"I'd better get back to work, packing. Bye, bye." Their good-bye was a very happy one.

Grandma and Mom were so delighted they sat staring at one another. "Can you believe it, Mother?" said Janet to her mother, "she is really coming home."

"Yes, and it's about time. This is where our girl belongs." Grandma pumped her fist in the air. "It's been three years, much too long. She will be much happier here with us, don't you agree, Janet?"

"I'm sure your right, Mother," replied Jill's mom; there was a hesitation in her mind though. "I will fix us a cup of tea—to celebrate." she got to her feet. She had to move for her mind, for some reason, was a bit unsettled. Grandma called after her as she went to the kitchen, "We probably should get her room ready for her don't you think?" Grandma felt she needed to get up, and do something too. As Janet fixed the tea she wondered, "How do we get her room any more ready than it already is?"

Bringing the two cups of tea into the living room, she was about to set them on the side table by each of their recliners when grandma quickly stood up and declared, "We must go through the dresser drawers in her room to make sure we haven't put any of our things in them and we must make her bed with nice clean linens."

Why, thought Janet? "She slept in her bed only one night!" But if that would make her mother feel like she was doing something special for Jill, then that is what they would do.

"We can dust and vacuum and be all ready for her homecoming— oh, I am so happy I don't know how to contain myself."

Jill's mom, still holding the two cups of tea was beginning to get into the same mind-set. "You're right, Mother. I'll take this tea back to kitchen to drink later and we will get busy."

Now she was feeling the same nervous energy, waiting for her daughter to come home. Out came the vacuum cleaner and dust cloths. Every surface had to polished and shined. Grandma went into her room and brought the new bedspread to Jill's room.

"Oh, Mother, are you going to give it to her before Christmas? Jill's mom couldn't believe her eyes.

"Yes, this is a better time. Jill will be pleased and surprised. She admired this spread when we were at the Bed and Bath store some time ago. I had them pack it away to mail here, in my name, when she wasn't looking."

"What a lovely thing to do, Mother," Janet went to her mother and gave her a loving hug and kiss on the cheek, "she will be so pleased. It just looks like it was made to go with this room. Doesn't it do the heart good to make someone happy, Jill, will so pleased. I just have to thank you it makes me so thrilled that you did this for her."

Grandma was equally happy she had made the decision. Janet loved her mother's smile, and was her mother actually blushing?

CHAPTER 25

The Big Decision

There were a lot of blank stares following Jack's question: "Do I stay or do I go?" It was almost amusing to watch Big Man's face, for it was unusual for him to be speechless. Faces shifted from Jack's face to Big Man's. There didn't seem to be any expressions from any of them that meant, Get rid of him. They were rather more general pleading looks as everyone was waiting for Big Man's answer. They were viewing him now in a different way—as a pastor.

Big Man looked around at all the fellows and Little Ma, and then at Jack. He said, "Jack, we need to have a talk, sort of in private." Jack answered by nodding. The others started leaving, going to their own places. Jack started to stand up, and Big Man touched his arm. "Let's just stay here. It won't matter to me if they hear what we talk about. Okay with you?"

"Yes, I would really prefer it that way too; I don't want anyone thinking we're ganging up on them and keeping secrets."

Jack was not sure how to go on; he needed more direction. "So do you have any more questions or perhaps suggestions for my being here?"

Big Man *was* a very big man, and he had a big voice to go with his stature. "I worry about this place we are illegally occupying, and as you experienced, I feel a fearful and fierce protection for the others. I'm not sure the Lord is going to keep making it possible for us to stay here—safely, that is. You know, you were here when the police came after us."

Jack could tell that all ears were open in the background. Their safety was at stake in staying in this place unlawfully.

"Well, Pastor—whoops … uh, well, you might as well get used to being addressed that way again. What *is* your name? I believe the Lord is talking to the both of us about this. It's been on my mind. Everyone here is like family. Why should they have to be separated and spread all over the place? I have been thinking over a plan of harmony and safety for us."

Big Man liked that Jack used the inclusive word "us" in talking about the group. "Okay, lay it on me, my friend. And my name is Benjamin; Pastor Ben is how my people—my congregation—referred to me.

"Sounds good to me, Pastor Ben. I inherited five hundred thousand dollars, but I don't want it for myself. I feel it should be used for the Lord's work. We maybe need to buy a tract of land for ourselves; what do you think?"

Jack saw tears well up in this huge, dear pastor's eyes. His chin quivered, and looking upward, he said, "What a marvelous God we serve.

Jack jumped up, threw his hands in the air, began to dance around and sang a little worship song he remembered:

> What a mighty God we serve;
> What a mighty God we serve.
> Heaven and earth adore you;
> Angels bow before you.
> What a mighty God we serve.

He almost felt as though he had been let out of some kind of prison. Jack grabbed Little Ma's hand and very gently, started dancing with her. She looked up adoringly at his face, thinking, "This is what some of ma sons couda been jes like." Jack couldn't stop dancing and singing. With a huge smile, Big Man grabbed Jack's wrist and Little Ma's; pulled Jack down to the stump as he helped Little Ma sit down. "Hey, you'll have to teach us that song and any other worship song you know. Okay? Let's get on with this though—Yes, we do serve a mighty God. Amen." He had to wipe his eyes with the back of his hands but was smiling a mighty big smile.

Jack settled down greatly relieved that everything was out in the open. It felt so good that he no longer had to be careful about being discovered while living among them. Looking around he could see they had already accepted him as who he was and why he was there. There was a general feeling of freedom among the group. They had occasionally discussed openly among themselves that there was something different about Jack—a difference they had come to respect,

"How about we call them together and share the possibility of this?" Speaking loudly Pastor Ben called out, "Somebody go get Squirrel."

As Squirrel came down from his perch high in the tree, where he did his spying to spot the arrival of the cops, he noticed most of the fellows looking at what they had been doing-- pretending to not be listening to Big Man and Jack's private talk.

"Okay, Little Ma, get the crew together and come back here. Jack and I have a plan we need to talk over with you all," said Big Man. He and Jack then revealed the unbelievable plan of a place for them to live lawfully—their own real home.

Some were fearful about all that was happening, but none wanted to pull out. Each began to name his or her abilities: The cook and assistant cook; the dishwasher for cook; a former wrestler and health trainer; an older man, though not as old as Little Ma; a man who made furniture from tree branches; two other men who had been farmers; one man had been a teacher in a private school; his assistant; "And we have you, Pastor, to take care of our spiritual needs," interjected Jack excitedly.

Jack became excited—"Pastor Ben we have a crew here that can take care of most of our needs—uh--legally," he added with a hint of a smile.

"Amen to that, and God has sent you to us Jack, to make it possible to put all these talents to work," Pastor Ben gratefully acknowledged his place and leaned close to Jack with his head down, "We'll get everyone one of these gents listening too and have them serving the Lord."

The fellows were getting excited; they began to offer their skills. Hub offered, "I used to work at a filling station and got pretty good at fixing cars," came this surprise when the quiet little man spoke up and offered his knowledge.

"I use to work at a tailor shop," said Karl another quiet fellow, with a sad voice, " but they had to downsize, and I was hired last so was the first to go."

"Wall ah use' ta rise kids. Rised nine of 'em. Outlived ever' one of 'em, bless their hides. Tha's why I ker for all ah you and ya call me Little Ma. Now jes remember, ya need someone to run things, an thas the Ma's job. Pa use' ta sit aroun' drinkin' his homebrew and smoking his pipe on the front porch. We got no front porch, so we don' need any pa here, ya hear?"

Sid said he used to drive Taxies but since they didn't have one he'd do somethin' else. Zeke just kept quiet. No one else spoke up.

"All these abilities we have among us," Pastor Ben said, "has been given to each of us as a gift from God, now each one of you think seriously about that and tell him thanks." Pastor Ben added, "Little

Ma, your gift may be the most important among us. We need to be kept in order and you do a good job, right fellows?"

Smiles and nods drifted among them as they looked at that precious little lady.

All eyes turned to the bushes near the side of the road as someone out of the blue, who looked homeless came strolling in. "Those are great plans that you are all cooking up. I'm Larry, and I'm a lawyer, and it sounds like you're going to need one—a good one."

Big Man was on his feet. The Lord had just that morning dealt with him and removed most of the fierceness and fear, for the group's safety, out of him.

Jack, too, was on his feet with wide-open eyes filled with surprise. "Hello! You're the mystery man I saw several times when I took some people from Pastor Ed's church to minister among the street people, right?"

"Well, I don't know how mysterious I am. My life's been plastered all over the news. But yes, I remember you from the same place and time. I've sort of kept my eye on you. I'm sure you don't remember me. I was in a couple of your classes in college, picking up two courses I needed."

The rest of the group began gathering around him, looking him over. Pastor Ben turned to everyone with a quizzical look and addressed everyone. "How do you feel about this fellow?"

Their glances were not very friendly, but they weren't hostile either. They were keeping their opinions to themselves for the time being. A close glance gave them a view of the scars on his face through his beard.

CHAPTER 26

Jill Asserts Herself

Their food pot was filled with a good assortment of vegetables plus another rabbit that one of the men had trapped. As Jack was looking for his plate and cup in his bedroll, he felt his cell phone vibrate. It took a while for him to dig it out, but he opened it on the last ring. "Hello, Jill! I'm so glad you called."

She yelled at him, saying, "I've been trying to get a hold of you for two days! Where have you been? Where are you? What are you doing? Are you with that woman?"

"You mean that eighty-eight-year-old lady with the injured ankle?"

"Oh … uh … well, yes, Jack?" Her voice was now soft and pleading. "I've moved back home with my mother and grandmother. Can you come by soon?"

"You tell me when, and I'll be there. Remember, though, my car was stolen, so I'm without wheels. Could you come out and get me? I'd like to go to the church to clean up, though, before seeing your mom and grandma. I really want to see you. I love you, and I've missed you so much. By the way, I read about you losing your dad, and I'm so sorry about that. He was a great fellow. Is your mom doing all right?"

"Mom is doing fairly well, thanks. Grandma has come to live with her. I can come get you. I sort of hate to face your pastor, though, after misunderstanding you and leaving like I did. Give me directions to your house." Her voice was soft, loving and low. Talking to her just melted his heart *and* posture.

"I don't live in a house, Jill, he returned in a tender voice."

"You don't what? What kind of game are you playing? What do you mean you don't live in a house? Are you--Jack, are you in a settlement? You'd better say no." Jill's volume began to rise. "Where do you live, Jack? Where am I going to find you—out on the street somewhere?" With voice coming still louder; "I hope you say no to that question." Her voice began to carry out into the woods. Jack held his phone away from his ear.

"Jill, calm down. Actually, we are camping at the edge of a farm in the woods, and it isn't really bad. We are camping along Route Thirty-One by the first overpass. Jill? Jill, are you crying? Jill--hello. Jill?" Jack shook his head back and forth--can you beat that? She hung up.

Jack dialed Jill's number, and it kept ringing, but she was not picking up. Now what?

"Is she a spiled brat, Pard?"

"Oh Little Ma, hi. What? A spoiled—don't call her that, Little Ma; I want to marry her. I'm going for a walk. I'll be back in a little while." Jack climbed the embankment and started walking off his frustration. About a mile down the interstate, he began asking Jesus what he should do about Jill. He didn't get an answer, so he turned and headed back. He got to the overpass and had just started down the embankment when he heard a horn. Looking down the road, he saw a nice car pull to the side of the road. Jill jumped out and ran toward him calling his name. He slipped and went sliding the rest of the way down the damp bank. He turned and saw Jill come tumbling after him, down the hill on the slick, wet grass, turning head over heels and screaming as she stumbled and rolled.

With wide-open eyes and outstretched arms, Jack tried to catch her at the bottom. She was covered with mud and grass, for it had rained the night before. Her hair was full of loose grass and weeds, and mud was covering her face. She soon had an audience of curious men and one limping elderly lady.

Little Ma was the first to speak, sizing up the situation and the crumpled body on the ground.

"Is this here thing yer prize, Pard?"

Jack was struggling to get Jill on her feet while brushing her off. She had mud up the length of her arms where she had tried to catch herself. She was spitting out grass, wiping her nose, and sweeping her long, thick hair out of her eyes.

Jill was in pretty sad shape while fighting and struggling to regain some composure. After shaking Jack's hands off, she peered at the group and finished off her popularity with just a few words: "Well, where did you find this sorry-looking bunch of heathens?"

Jack cringed at her using that phrase again.

There was total silence except for the sound of cars rushing by on the highway. Everyone was too stunned to say anything. From the back came someone's laughter. It soon turned into an uncontrollable roar. Big Man came weaving through the crowd of men, holding his hand out to Jill. The kind look on his face wilted her anger. She put her hand in his and let him lead her over to the best chair—the only chair-- they had. As he gazed at her, softly chuckling, with love in his eyes, she looked down at herself and began to laugh too, then her laughter turned into more tears and wailing.

Big Man went down on one knee and spoke magic words to her, "I do believe the Lord has sent an angel to us and clothed her to look like us so we wouldn't be afraid. Welcome, my dear."

Jack went to her and sat on the stump close by. "Thanks for coming, Jill. I want to introduce you to one of the nicest bunch of people on God's green earth. Little Ma and fellows, I proudly present the girl I hope to marry very soon—and no wisecracks. I just hope she'll have me." He, too, went down on one knee. He took hold of her hand and, with utmost sincerity, said, "Jill, darling, will you marry me? And if you're too startled to answer right now, you can give me your answer later. I love you with all my heart and will work the rest of my life to give you a happy life with me. I know I will never be able to apologize enough for my stupidity while we were in college. Too late I realized how I should have explained about the offer of the newspaper job and the work it was going to take to get the credits I would need for the job. Open up this crazy, mixed-up heart of mine, Jill, so I can pour out the love and appreciation I feel for you. Will you marry me Sweetheart?"

"No--oh, I mean yes, but no—oh, Jack, I look so awful. Maybe later, if that's all right."

Streams of tears were running down her face again. Little Ma limped over to the bag of supplies that Jack had brought from the drugstore, walked over to Jill and wiped her tears with a sterile pad.

"Jack, ya dummy, this here gal needs yer arms around her. Come here, honey bug." She put her arms around Jill's shoulders and said, "There, there, now, dearie. Everything's gonna be jes fine; you wait an' see."

Jill willingly melted into Little Ma's bony arms and kissed her on the cheek. Little Ma was crying too. Jill reached for the now damp sterile pad and wiped Little Ma's tears.

Jill's hair was such a mess. Little Ma went for her big-toothed comb. Jill closed her eyes and relaxed as her hair was lovingly combed to show its beautiful length and dark waves, in spite of what it had been through. Jack just watched with entranced amazement. "A woman can sure confuse a guy."

As best as they could, everyone helped Jill clean up somewhat, urged her to stay for supper, fed her a tasty plate of food from the boiling pot, then bade her good-bye, telling her to come back again. Jack helped her up the embankment. They held one another in their arms momentarily on the busy highway and kissed one another. Horns blew, whistles sounded, and one car swerved dangerously with squealing brakes. "Guess we'd better get off stage, right?" she said.

"I love you Jill," Jack replied. Her answer was breathless as she returned the same tender endearment. Jill climbed into her car and was soon on her way home in a much better frame of mind.

When all was settled for the evening, Jack got out his French harp and began to play softly. As he played their favorite hymn, Pastor Ben began to sing. One at a time, others joined in.

> Amazing Grace, how sweet the sound
> That saved a wretch like me;
> I once was lost but now am found,
> Was blind, but now I see....

Pastor Ben gave them a short sermon about Jesus' commandment to love one another and then held up his hand to bless them in the name of the Father, Son, and Holy Spirit. They retired that evening with the peace of God in their hearts.

Shorty soon had his church, and Jack murmured a grateful "Thank You, Lord God."

Little Ma felt a surge of love in her whole being.

Big Man, Pastor Ben, slowly shook his head as he bent over in praise. "Is this where You wanted me, Lord?" he asked. He prayed for each person of the group, including Jill.

He prayed for the group and what the Lord had in his plan for each one of them. "Help them all be where You want them, Lord, and help them carry out Your plan in that place. Amen."

Jill drove home with a smile on her face and Wedding Bells pealing in her heart. She knew where she would go to find her wedding gown. She thought her heart would burst with happiness, "Thank you Lord. Thank You for bringing Jack and I back together. Help me, so I just keep trusting You. Please keep me in Your will. I've been so willful and rebellious. Forgive me, Lord. Amen."